D0746029

Smoked

Garry Ryan

SMOKED

✕

A Detective Lane Mystery

NeWest Press

COPYRIGHT © GARRY RYAN 2010

✕

LIBRARY AND ARCHIVES CANADA CATALOGUING IN PUBLICATION

Ryan, Garry, 1953–
    Smoked / Garry Ryan.

Also available in electronic format.
ISBN 978-1-897126-62-2

    I. Title.

PS8635.Y354S62   2010 C813'.6   C2009-906221-6

✕

Editor for the Board: Douglas Barbour
Cover and interior design: Natalie Olsen, Kisscut Design
Author photo: Karma Ryan
Copyediting: NJ Brown
Proofreading: Paul Matwychuk

Canada Council for the Arts   Conseil des Arts du Canada   Canadian Heritage   Patrimoine canadien   Alberta Foundation for the Arts   edmonton arts council

NeWest Press acknowledges the support of the Canada Council for the Arts, the Alberta Foundation for the Arts, and the Edmonton Arts Council for our publishing program. We acknowledge the financial support of the Government of Canada through the Canada Book Fund for our publishing activities.

NEWEST PRESS

#201, 8540–109 Street
Edmonton, Alberta T6G 1E6
780.432.9427
www.newestpress.com

No bison were harmed in the making of this book.

printed and bound in Canada   1 2 3 4 5 13 12 11 10

FOR

ALLAN,

DEBBIE,

COLE,

DAYNA

chapter 1

"Where is she?" Arthur looked at the phone, expecting it to ring.

Lane looked at the clock; it read 3:30 AM. "I have no idea." He rubbed at the remains of his ear lobe. A drunken, abusive husband had bitten off the rest during a domestic dispute call.

Arthur pulled the curtain back and looked out the window of their front-to-back split-level home. The light outside the front door highlighted his pear-shaped silhouette. "Matt didn't shovel the sidewalk."

"Want me to do it?" In an attempt to wake up, Lane rubbed his face with his open palm. *Matt must be hoping the sun will come out and clear away the snow. There's warmer weather in the forecast,* he thought.

Arthur let the curtain close and turned to face Lane. "No."

Roz's nails tapped the floor. She looked at Lane, yawned, and stretched with her paws way out front so that her back and tail curled. Lane rubbed her head and the thick fur behind her ears. She wagged her tail in thanks.

"Want me to make some coffee?" Lane asked as he went into the kitchen.

"Sure." Arthur sat on the couch. Roz moved over and sat next to him.

When the knock came, the volume and the force of it told Lane what and who to expect.

Unfortunately, Arthur opened the door before Lane could get to it. "Oh no!" His face paled as he stepped back from the door.

Lane moved past Arthur. He looked at Christine's face, or, actually, the top of her head and its fresh dye job. Today, her natural black was a silver azure. There was no makeup on her face. Lane put his hand on her shoulder.

She looked at him.

He studied her eyes to read what words might not tell him.

Christine looked back at him with a mixture of embarrassment and rage. She shrugged his hand away.

Good, no permanent damage and no drugs, Lane thought.

He recognized the officer dressed in his blues. Noted checked his nametag: McTavish. Lane looked at the officer's face. The intense lights at the front door illuminated McTavish's salt and pepper hair. "Come in," Lane said.

Christine brushed past Lane. McTavish handed Christine's backpack to her uncle.

"Are you okay?" Arthur asked her as she unlaced the combat boots she'd bought with money from her first job.

Christine didn't answer. Instead, she sat on the couch and glared at each of them in turn.

"Cup of coffee?" Lane asked McTavish.

"That would be nice," McTavish said.

"Please, sit down." Lane indicated the living room. "Christine? You want a coffee?" He moved into the kitchen.

"Yep. And, by the way, this is bullshit!"

Lane poked his head back into the living room to glare at Christine.

She closed her mouth.

A minute later, Lane brought out a tray with four coffees, milk, brown sugar, and spoons. He set the tray on the coffee table so each of them could doctor their drinks. Then, they sat at opposite corners of the living room and studied one another.

"Well, now that everyone has talked my ear off." Arthur

attempted to make a joke and shrugged his round shoulders when it flopped.

Lane looked at McTavish, remembering their last meeting. Lane thought, *He's probably remembering the same thing. He looks a little greyer since the blockade.*

McTavish said. "When I asked her where she lived, and who she lived with, I remembered your name. What's the relationship?"

"I'm her uncle." Lane nodded at Arthur, who was getting some colour back in his face. "We're legal guardians."

McTavish nodded, gripping the cup. It disappeared in his large hands.

"Christine, what happened?" Lane asked.

Christine crossed her arms under her breasts then crossed one leg over the other.

"The facts," he said.

"I was in Kensington. I took my can of paint out and tagged a dumpster. He," Christine nodded in McTavish's direction without making eye contact, "cuffed me, put me in the back of his car, asked me some questions, and brought me here."

Lane looked at McTavish.

"That's exactly what happened." McTavish went back to sipping his coffee and watching.

Lane looked at Christine. *What do I say next?* he thought.

"How come this is bullshit?" McTavish asked, recalling Christine's earlier words.

"The whole idea is." Christine looked at Lane to gauge his reaction.

"What idea is that?" Arthur leaned forward.

Lane noted the dark circles under Arthur's eyes.

"The idea that you can't say what you think. Can't write what you think. Somebody is always telling you what to say. What to think. Usually it's hypocritical men telling me how to live my life. That's bullshit." Christine took a sip of her coffee and looked over her cup at the men, daring one of them to disagree.

"You and I agree so far as restrictions on freedom of speech go," McTavish said.

Arthur turned to McTavish. "You agree with her?"

"Of course. Saying what you think, especially when you write it down, is probably the best way for anyone in our society to get into trouble." McTavish put his empty cup on the tray.

Lane looked at McTavish, then at Christine. "So, what are our choices?"

"We've had lots of complaints from Kensington businesses about graffiti. Most don't like having their property tagged. If Christine wants to clean up her tags, there won't be any charges. If she chooses to leave them, then she'll be charged."

"See what I mean? It's bullshit!" Christine shook her head. "You guys don't understand a damned thing!"

McTavish stood up. "What's it gonna be?"

"Saturday morning okay for us to clean up?" Lane asked.

"No problem." McTavish turned to Christine. "How many did you tag?"

"Twelve or thirteen."

McTavish went to the door. "Thanks for the coffee." He opened the door and stepped outside.

Lane followed him. He shivered and tucked his hands under his armpits. "McTavish?"

The officer turned and smiled.

"Thanks." Lane held out his hand.

McTavish shook it. His grip was firm. "Thank you. I've seen what happens to kids who end up on the street. One of my nephews ran away last winter. It was the coldest night of the year. He got frostbite. Almost lost all of his fingers."

The officer stepped down to his car. He turned as he got to the car, looked back at Lane, hesitated, and went back up the steps. "Might be a good idea to keep your eyes and ears open the next little while."

Lane cocked his head to one side. "What's up?"

"Looks like we're getting a new chief." McTavish looked past Lane to see if anyone was hanging around the front door. "You know him. The guy who lives to network."

"Smoke?" Lane watched McTavish's eyes.

McTavish nodded. "Watch your back." He turned, walked down the steps, got into the car, and drove away.

Lane came inside just in time to see Christine run up the stairs and slam the door to her room. "What happened?"

"I said, 'When are we going to talk about this?' She yelled at me and ran upstairs." Arthur shrugged his shoulders. "What time do you have to be at work?"

Lane looked at the grandfather clock. "A couple of hours."

×

The phone rang as Lane pulled on a shirt. He picked up the receiver before it could wake Arthur. "Hello?" Lane looked down and saw water soaking through the blue fabric of his shirt where he hadn't completely dried after the shower.

"It's me," Harper said. "We've got a missing woman."

"Any specifics?" Lane pulled on socks, then grabbed his keys and cash from the dresser.

"She's twenty-one. Reported missing by her parents. She left for work Monday morning. That's the last time they saw her. She phoned home at lunch to say she'd be home for supper. When her parents drove to her office, the daughter's car was there. The first place we need to go is a dental office a few kilometres from your house. It's called Rockwell Sedation Dentistry."

Lane looked out the window. The sky was gradually turning from purple to pink. "That's right next to Kuldeep's coffee shop," he said. "We need to pay both of them a visit. Is the dentist open yet?"

"In an hour. I'll pick you up in twenty." Harper hung up. Lane put the phone down.

"What are we going to do about Christine?" Arthur was facing away from Lane, as if he were speaking to the wall.

"Sorry I woke you." Lane pulled on his sports jacket.

Arthur rolled over. "Well?"

"What time does she get home from class?"

"Four-thirty or five." Arthur put his feet on the floor.

"We'll sit down when I get home." Lane made for the door.

"Better put your pants on." Arthur rolled over.

Twenty-five minutes later, Lane and Harper pulled up in front of Kuldeep's coffee shop. Lane turned and looked at the mountains as he stepped out of the Chev. They were heavy with snow, waiting for the spring sun and resultant runoff.

Inside the shop, Lane closed his eyes and imagined the first sip of coffee. *Kuldeep makes a good cup,* he thought.

"The usual?" Kuldeep had her black hair pulled back into a bun.

"Yep," Harper said.

Lane looked around. The shop was empty. He sat down next to the front window where he could keep an eye on the comings and goings outside. "Do you go to the dentist next door?" Kuldeep poked her head around from behind the espresso machine. "What?"

"Do you go next door for dental work?"

Kuldeep's smile died. "No way." She went back to making coffee.

Harper sat down. He studied Lane's face. "What happened to you?"

"Remember McTavish?" Lane rubbed his eyes.

"The tactical guy?"

Lane nodded. "He brought Christine home this morning at about three o'clock. She'd been tagging dumpsters."

Kuldeep brought them their coffees. "There you go." She set them down on the table.

"Do the people who work at the dentist's office come here?" Harper asked.

Kuldeep paused and looked at each of them in turn. "A few."

How come her defenses are up all of a sudden? Lane wondered. *She must hate going to the dentist.*

"Apparently, a dental assistant named Jennifer didn't make it home last night." Harper looked at Lane, then looked away.

He notices the change in Kuldeep too, Lane thought.

"Jennifer?" Kuldeep looked outside at a patron getting out of his Cadillac.

"Yes," Lane said.

"She came in around three o'clock yesterday afternoon. I could see that she had been crying. She ordered a large coffee and went back to the office." Kuldeep watched the patron adjust his tie, button his blue suit jacket, and approach the door.

"How come you don't send your family next door for their dental work?" Lane asked.

Kuldeep's eyes opened wide. "I'm not crazy."

The door opened. The patron in the navy blue suit stepped inside. Kuldeep went back behind the counter.

A black, late-model Mercedes pulled into the parking lot and stopped to the west of the coffee shop. Lane watched as the driver got out. He had a goatee, round face, and close-cropped blond hair.

"What's happened to the chief?" Lane waited for an answer as Harper put down his cup.

"She's going in for a bypass. Smoke's the acting chief until she's back." Harper shook his head.

"What's the long face about? Last night I was told Smoke was the new chief and got a warning to watch my back."

Harper frowned. A crease ran across his forehead. He rubbed the back of his hand across his mouth. "Smoke's a climber. Well-connected politically. Meets regularly with Bishop Paul, local businessmen, and like-minded cops. They have a scotch drinkers' night once a month. Cops who join the club have been the people getting all the promotions lately."

"I ran into him once or twice when I was starting out," Lane said.

"And?" Harper waited while Lane looked out the window.

"My first year on the force we were trying to catch this guy on a motorcycle. He would bait cops by stunting right in front of them. A chase would ensue. He'd escape down a bike trail or he'd go cross-country. Most of it happened on this side of the river. One afternoon, the rider got caught. I was late getting there. I could see Smoke holding back traffic and bystanders. When the arresting officers brought the rider back, he had a bloody nose and one of his eyes was swollen. He was holding his ribs. The officers took him to the hospital and two of his ribs were broken. The officers said he fell off his bike while trying to escape. I looked at the bike. There was no evidence of recent damage to it." Lane continued to stare through the window into the past.

"So, you think the arresting officers laid a few licks on the motorcycle rider?" Harper asked.

Lane nodded. "And the rider refused to lay charges."

"What's this got to do with Smoke?" Harper asked.

"I went to him and explained about the bike. He shrugged it off and said, 'Don't ask too many questions.' A few years later we were both up for a detective's job. I got it. A week later, I was outed." Lane looked directly at Harper.

"You think it was Smoke?" Harper looked across at a customer who was waiting for his coffee.

Lane nodded. "I was being taught a lesson for getting the job he wanted."

"How do you know it was him?" Harper asked.

"You know when you go into a room and someone has been smoking, but no one has a cigarette? No one will own up to it. It's like that. There's the smell of smoke in the air but everyone's acting innocent. Still, it stinks, and it smelled strongest around the new chief."

Harper chewed at his lip. "When I worked in the chief's office, Smoke had a partner who quit the force. The chief interviewed her. It was one of those rare times the chief confided in me. She said, 'Smoke's partner was too scared to tell me why she's quitting. She just said she wanted out.' By that time Smoke had made quite a few political connections. He was on his way up."

"There always seems to be the scent of back-room deals, good ol' boys, and twelve-year-old scotch around Smoke," Lane said.

Harper turned his head and watched Kuldeep. "There you go," she said and handed a customer his coffee. As the customer left, she leaned to look out the window. Kuldeep made eye contact with Harper then cocked her head to the right. Harper lifted his chin. "Come on," he said to Lane. "Our man's arrived." He stood and picked up his coffee.

Lane followed Harper out the door.

The driver of a black Mercedes wore black gloves and a black leather jacket. He pointed his key at the lock of the dental office.

"Hello." Harper waited until the man turned.

Lane watched the man's eyes.

"I'm Detective Harper and this is Detective Lane." Harper pointed at Lane with his coffee cup.

Lane tried to study the man's reaction, but there wasn't one. *Interesting,* Lane thought.

"Dr. Joseph Jones." Jones turned his back, opened the door, stepped inside, and hooked his foot around the metal doorframe to hold it open. "Come in."

They followed him past a copper waterfall stretching from floor to ceiling. The carpets were burgundy and the walls sea foam. Paintings of idyllic homes surrounded by flowers and white fences were carefully aligned on either side of the waterfall. The scent of lavender and aftershave followed in Jones' wake.

Lane watched Dr. Jones as he threw his shoulders back to walk tall at five-foot-six. He opened an office and stood outside as Lane and Harper went inside. Jones followed them in, closed the door behind them, hung up his jacket, and sat behind a polished black mahogany desk.

Putting us in our place. Next he'll try and show us how busy he is by making us wait here, Lane thought. Before Jones could play the waiting game, Lane said. "We understand that Jennifer Towers is one of your employees. Are you aware that she's missing?"

Jones smiled. "Yes, to both statements. And we're really worried that she might have been hurt. She really is a nice young woman. A real asset to the practice."

"We would appreciate any information you can give us." Lane stared at Jones, who looked back with an expression Lane couldn't decipher.

Jones smiled. "There's not much to tell, I'm afraid. I didn't see her leave work. I saw her briefly Monday afternoon. She seemed fine. I didn't see her leave. I worked late." His smile was replaced by a puzzled frown.

Lane watched Jones' eyes. *Something doesn't add up here,* he thought. *The eyes and the voice are sending different messages.*

"Her parents reported her missing. Her car was found

parked outside in *your* parking lot." Harper used 'your' on purpose to see if it would provoke a reaction.

Jones frowned some more. "She's one of our best assistants. We'd be lost without her. We've really come to rely on her. I hope she turns up soon."

It all sounds rehearsed, Lane thought.

"Do you have any idea where she might have gone after work?" Harper asked as he lifted his nose and sniffed the air.

"None. I saw her during the course of the day, and noticed nothing unusual." Jones leaned back in his chair, crossing an ankle over his knee.

"Was anyone working late with you?" Lane asked.

Jones smiled. "No. I sometimes work alone to get my paperwork done. It was one of those nights. I got home around eight. My wife and daughters can vouch for me after that."

"We'd like to wait and interview your staff." Harper made it sound like a fait accompli.

"Of course. The staff should be here within the next fifteen minutes. We'll do everything we can to help get Jennifer safely back to her family." Dr. Jones stood up. As he shook Harper's hand, Lane studied the puzzled half-smile on the doctor's face.

Harper asked, "What's that smell? It's sweet."

"I don't smell anything. You must be mistaken." Jones smiled.

Lane headed for the waiting room. He sat down and Harper sat next to him.

"Picking up odd vibes?" Lane asked.

Harper nodded. "You betcha."

They turned at the sound of a key opening the lock. A woman dressed in yellows and whites stepped in. She was approximately five-foot-four, with short brown hair and a sumo wrestler's physique. She locked the door, turned, and let out a tiny chirp as her hand went to her mouth.

"Sorry we startled you." Lane stood and offered his hand. "I'm Detective Lane and this is Detective Harper."

The woman kept her hand over her mouth. Her eyes blinked several times, revealing yellow eyeshadow.

Lane read her nametag. "You're Ramona?"

Ramona took her hand away from her mouth. "How'd you know that?"

Harper pointed at her nametag.

She covered her tag with her hand. "Jennifer lied."

"About what?" Lane asked.

"About Doctor Joe. Jennifer strutted around the office, advertising what God gave her." Ramona leaned closer to Harper. "She was only here a month, you know."

"Do any other dentists work here?" Lane decided he'd wait for Ramona to tell them what she thought Jennifer had lied about.

"Dr. Stephen. He and Dr. Joe have been working together for five years." Ramona walked over to her receptionist command centre. It provided an effective barrier between her and the detectives. She took a breath, put her hand to her throat, fluttered her eyelashes, and smiled at them.

"What time did Jennifer leave Monday?" Harper stood up and set his pocket computer on the counter.

"I don't know. She wasn't talking to me. She was still here when I left." Ramona sat in her chair.

"How come she wasn't talking to you?" Lane stood next to Harper.

"Because I told her to button up her blouse. Some of the male patients were becoming quite distracted." Ramona pursed her lips and shook her head.

"You had complaints about her from the patients?" Lane asked.

"No. But you could see the men's eyes when they came in. Watching the way she traipsed around here in her tight little uniform." Ramona rolled her eyes. "That's why I knew she was lying."

"About what?" Harper looked up from his computer.

"About what the patient said." Ramona looked at them as if they should already know what she was talking about.

"What did the patient say?" Lane looked over his shoulder as a patient opened the door.

"I'm not talking about that!" Ramona looked over Lane's shoulder at the man who was shutting the door.

"Could you tell us what time Jennifer left here on Monday?" Harper smiled at the patient, who attempted to smile back.

Ramona flipped pages in her appointment book. "Don't know exactly, but her last appointment was at three."

"Was it for a cleaning?" Lane asked.

Ramona stuck her finger on the page. "Yes." She looked away and addressed the patient. "Now, Mr. Francis, it's time for your appointment."

"One more question." Lane held eye contact with Ramona. "How long would that appointment have taken?"

Ramona said, "Forty minutes." She flapped a hand at Mr. Francis. "Come right this way."

$\times$

"Madeline?"

She felt his hand on her shoulder and was immediately awake. Maddy looked around. The classroom was empty. Sunlight drew a line through the room. Dread almost overwhelmed her. She felt her eyes filling with tears.

"You fell asleep and class is over." Mr. Hugh watched her closely.

Maddy hated it when he looked at her like that. *He can see right through me. I'm afraid he'll make me talk.* Maddy sat up. She stood up and reached for her black jacket. "Am I late for my next class?"

"Don't worry; I'll write you a note if you need one." Hugh stepped back, still watching her.

Maddy picked up her books and stuffed them into her bag.

"How come you're so tired?" he asked.

"My little sister…" She stopped herself and thought, *Don't go there!*

Hugh waited for her to go on. He scratched his white beard.

You're just too smart for an old man, she thought. "I'm late," she said.

"Take care," he said. "And get some sleep."

"Whatever you say." Maddy hefted her bag and left.

×

"How did rehearsal go?" Lane asked.

Matt blew his nose and put the tissue in his pocket. He shrugged, put on his seat belt, leaned his head back, and closed his eyes. "Fine."

"Feeling okay?" Lane stopped the car, waiting for traffic at the exit to the high-school parking lot to clear.

"I'm getting a cold. The first performance is next week." Matt leaned forward to wave at a girl wearing a white winter jacket and blue jeans.

Lane pulled out into the street. He glanced at Matt, who wore a scarf, a tight-fitting grey toque, a black greatcoat he'd purchased at a secondhand store, and blue jeans. Matt had gone through a wide variety of styles over the last two or three months as he tried on an actor's skin.

Lane said, "Can't wait to see the play."

"Really?" Matt looked at Lane.

"Of course." Lane stopped at the lights. "Who's the girl?"

"Carol." Matt looked away.

"She in the play?" Lane tried not to notice Matt's sudden

nervousness, or the embarrassment that shaded his neck and worked its way to his scalp.

"She's one of the crew." Matt's breath fogged the passenger window.

"Do you miss hockey?" Lane accelerated as the light turned green. He turned north on Shaganappi Trail. *Traffic is lighter now that it's almost seven,* he thought.

Matt looked at Lane. "Do you?"

"I miss seeing you on the ice." *Now, that surprised me,* Lane thought. "And I miss how I feel when I'm skating."

Matt smiled. "Never thought you'd miss hockey."

"Supper should be on when we get home. It'll be nice to relax for a few minutes."

"Good luck," Matt shook his head.

"What do you mean?"

Matt shook his head again. "There's always some kinda drama at home."

They walked in the door fifteen minutes later.

"You're gonna kick me out anyway, so I might as well leave!" Christine pushed past Lane and Matt as they took off their shoes.

They looked at one another.

Christine hooked the backpack over her shoulder, shoved her feet into running shoes, and slammed the door behind her.

"She failed a Math test." Arthur's eyes told the sad story of his evening. He focused vaguely on Lane.

Lane shrugged. "That's not so bad."

"She came in the door about two hours ago." Arthur sat on the couch.

The dog scratched at the back door. Matt went to open it. He bent to wipe the snow from her paws.

"Aren't you going after her?" Arthur asked Lane.

"No." Lane took his winter coat off and hung it in the closet.

"But it's cold out." Arthur stood up, pulled back the drapes, and looked outside.

"Maybe she'll cool off sooner." Lane rubbed his hands together to warm them.

Arthur didn't look convinced. "Supper's ready," he said.

Roz scampered inside, followed by Matt.

Five minutes later, they sat down to dinner. Arthur's pattern was to take a mouthful, look at the back door, look at Christine's empty chair, and begin chewing. "Aren't you worried?" he asked.

"She left her stuff here. She'll be back," Lane said.

Roz barked.

They heard a key in the front door lock.

Arthur stood up.

Christine stepped inside. Her face was red from the wind.

"The food is still hot." Lane felt his stomach twist into knots. His appetite disappeared.

Arthur took Christine's coat. She washed her hands in the kitchen sink and sat down at the table. "I want to try to get in touch with my father."

Arthur handed her the chicken. Lane passed the rice. They ate the remainder of the meal in silence.

chapter 2

"Recently, she and her boyfriend broke it off. Apparently, he's been hanging around after work waiting to talk with her." Harper wrapped his hands around the steering wheel as they coasted down the hill. His kubasa fingers gave the impression he was incapable of being delicate. His black hair was greying a bit. He wore sunglasses to shield his eyes from the white glare of sunshine on melting snow. Harper turned on the wipers to clear the spray left by the vehicle in front of them. Outside, the river valley stretched west and east. The spring snowfall had painted the grass on the far side of the valley in an emerald green that peered out from under a layer of white. "You look like hell, by the way," Harper said to Lane.

Lane closed his eyes, hoping they'd stop for another cup of coffee before meeting the ex-boyfriend. "What's his name?"

"James Sanders. Works at City Cycle in Bowness." Harper turned left, then left again. They paralleled the railway tracks before turning onto the bridge.

Lane looked down into the water. It was running brown. The shrubbery on the island in the middle of the Bow River leaned with the current. "Water's pretty high."

"It's snowing and melting in the mountains." Harper looked ahead to the three-way stop on the far side of the river.

It took another five minutes to get to the motorcycle shop.

Lane opened the front door of City Cycle. The inside smelled of rubber, oil, leather, and freshly machined metal. They looked around at the motorcycles and four-wheelers on display.

Toys for boys, Lane thought.

"Always wanted one of these." Harper said as he walked over to a touring bike.

"Can I help?" asked a woman wearing jeans and a sleeveless red blouse. Her hair was shoulder-length and black.

Lane noted the hitch in her walk. He looked for tattoos but couldn't see any. "I'm Detective Lane, and this is Detective Harper."

The woman put her hands on her hips.

"And, you are?" Harper asked.

"Carley." She shrugged as she said her name.

Lane studied her as she put her weight on one leg.

"We need to talk with James Sanders." Harper said as he moved to stand next to Lane.

"He in trouble?" Carley's tone of voice had gone from welcoming to challenging.

Lane thought, *It's time to change the way this conversation is going.* "How did you lose your leg?" he asked.

Carley cocked her head to one side. "How'd you know?"

Lane shrugged. *I just know,* he thought.

"Motorcycle accident on the highway. I was eighteen. Lost it just below the knee. Want to see?" Carley bent over to lift her pant leg.

"We would really like to see James." Lane kept his tone even so there was nothing but sincerity in his voice.

Carley stood up and stared back at Lane. "He's upset. He had nothing to do with Jenny's disappearance. You won't believe me, but that's the truth."

"We need to hear that from him," Harper said.

"You can use my office." Carley turned and they followed her to a metal spiral staircase. She took the stairs one at a time. At the top, they stood eye-to-eye with antique motorcycles lined up along a balcony outside of the office. Once inside the office she said, "Have a seat. Coffee's there." She pointed at a carafe sitting atop the counter running under windows that looked down on the sales floor. "Help yourself. I'll get James."

Lane and Harper fixed their coffees. Lane sat. Harper stood so he could look down at the motorcycles.

Harper said, "It's awfully quiet all of a sudden."

Lane took a sip of coffee and closed his eyes. *I hope I can get some sleep tonight,* he thought.

"Here he comes."

There was the ring of feet on the metal steps of the stairway.

Harper stood to one side as a young man walked into the office.

Lane stood. "James Sanders?"

James nodded. His hair was close cut. A black T-shirt covered a barrel chest. He wore black jeans and stood a head shorter than either of the detectives.

Harper closed the door.

James' face flushed red as he looked up at Harper.

Lane read James' reaction and nodded at Harper to sit down.

James sat on the edge of the desk.

"I'm Detective Harper and this is Detective Lane." Harper sat, took a sip of coffee, and studied James.

"You had a relationship with Jennifer Towers?" Lane studied James' body language and read the tension there.

James nodded. "Yep."

"The relationship ended recently?" Lane watched as James leaned back on the desk.

"We had a fight."

"You're aware she's missing?" Harper seemed to be studying his coffee cup.

Lane thought, *Listen carefully for a change in James' tone of voice.*

James scratched his head like he wanted to strip away bits of flesh. "We were going to make up. But that's not why you're here, is it?"

"We want to locate her." Lane watched James' eyes fill with tears.

"And you think that because I'm the ex-boyfriend I'm responsible! That I couldn't accept the fact that she broke up with me. You know, the old stereotype—if I couldn't have her, then no one could." James stood up. "You cops are so stupid!"

Harper began to stand.

Lane saw James' eyes switch from rage to fear.

James lunged at Harper with the palm of his right-hand pushing forward, propelling Harper back into his chair.

Harper leaned into the blow, all arms and legs, trying to get back on his feet without spilling his coffee. James shoved him back into the chair again.

Lane grabbed for James' arm.

The right angles of the back of Harper's chair hit the safety glass. It bowed and sang before exploding and cascading into pebbles.

James was off balance, but managed to kick Lane in the face and Harper in the belly.

Coffee splashed against the wall.

James ran out the door.

Stunned by the blow, Lane fell back into the corner. He sat up, put his hand to his face and crawled to his feet.

Harper was on his back, taking in great gulps of air. Lane offered his hand. Harper pushed it away. Lane rushed down the spiral staircase. There was no sign of Sanders below.

Lane hit the floor at the bottom of the staircase, and his knees nearly buckled. He regained his balance and ran down a hallway leading to the back of the shop, where he found a door opening to the alley. Outside, two men looked at each other and then at the detective. A woman on a bicycle coasted past them. Lane could hear the high-pitched acceleration of a motorcycle racing toward the city centre.

Harper came out the door. He leaned against the wall, looked at Lane, and they ran in opposite directions.

Carley was sweeping up glass when they returned several minutes later. Harper stood at the bottom of the staircase and shook bits of glass from his hair and shoulders.

Lane walked up to Carley, who handed him a bag of ice. "Comes in handy around here. Always keep some in the fridge." She leaned on the push broom.

Lane eased the ice up against his eye.

She smiled at him. "You probably still won't listen to me, but here's the truth. James loved that girl. I know all about the kind of men who hurt women. James isn't that kind. He'll tangle with you two, but there's no way he would have hurt her."

"Tell that to him." Lane took the ice from his eye and pointed at Harper.

"You guys cornered him," Carley said.

"And what would he do to Jennifer if she cornered him?" Lane asked.

Carley leaned to sweep the glass into a pile. "I knew you wouldn't listen."

To Lane, her voice sounded more resigned than accusatory.

"We need his address," Harper said.

×

"It'll take a week to get that glass out of your hair." Lane drove as Harper looked in the mirror and picked crumbs of glass from his clothing and scalp and flicked the bits out the window.

"Should've seen it coming." Harper rolled a booger-sized bit of glass between his thumb and forefinger.

"My hindsight is very accurate too."

"There'll be more than a few laughs about this. Two cops beat up by one suspect. And that eye of yours is going to be plenty of pretty colours in a day or two." Harper looked at the swelling above and below Lane's left eye.

"Still think we should go see the parents, looking like this?" Lane stopped at a red light just below the Children's Hospital. The building's red and yellow squares gave the impression that it was constructed of a child's building blocks.

"I already phoned the parents. Just after we put out the call on James Sanders. Don't see how we can put it off." Harper straightened his collar.

The Towers' residence was a brick bungalow just north of a golf course. Lane parked out front. The driveway was filled with two late-model Fords. One was a sedan, the other a pickup.

Harper got out, gingerly removing more glass from his hair. He looked at Lane. "How do you want to handle this?"

"At this point, we probably need to listen more than anything else." Lane knocked on the front door.

Harper stood behind him on the bottom step.

Lane looked down on Harper to see particles of glass reflected in his hair and on his shoulders. The door opened. Lane turned.

The woman studied Lane through the glass of the storm door.

"I'm Detective Lane, and this is Detective Harper. We'd like to ask some questions about Jennifer Towers. Are you her mother?" *She looks like she hasn't slept in weeks,* Lane thought.

"Yes, I'm her mother, MaryAnne. Come in." She stepped back into the shadows as Lane opened the door.

It took a moment for Lane's eyes to adjust to the lack of light in the front room. MaryAnne stood nearly five feet tall. Her short black hair was flattened on the left side.

"Is there any news?" she asked.

Lane heard emptiness in her voice. "Not yet." He looked around the living room, where pictures of Jennifer's life covered one wall. He looked at MaryAnne Towers as it dawned on him that Jennifer was an only child.

"Tea? Coffee?" MaryAnne asked while walking toward the kitchen.

"What is easy for you?" Harper asked her.

"My Jennifer back." MaryAnne didn't bother looking back.

They followed her into the kitchen.

Lane looked back as an oak floorboard creaked.

"Who are you?" The man in the hall stood over six feet tall. He had a full head of red hair.

"They're detectives, Don." MaryAnne turned on the tap to fill the coffee pot.

"Any news?" There was hope in Don's voice.

"Not yet." Harper shrugged.

Don sat at the kitchen table. "Sit down."

Lane and Harper sat on either side of him. The coffee maker sputtered. The scent of arabica beans filled the room.

MaryAnne turned around. "This is not like her. She always phones."

Don asked, "Did you talk with her boyfriend?"

"James Sanders?" Harper asked, then looked at Lane.

Don nodded. "That's right."

"Less than an hour ago," Lane said.

Don got up, then returned with spoons, sugar, and milk. He sat down, got up again, and returned with four coffee cups.

"It didn't go well." MaryAnne said.

Lane noticed that it was a statement rather than a question. He looked closely at Jennifer's mother.

"You have swelling around your eye. Your partner's got bits of glass in his hair and on his clothes." MaryAnne sat.

Harper checked one shoulder of his sports jacket then the other.

"What was their relationship like?" Lane asked.

Don and MaryAnne looked at one another.

Don said, "I didn't like his short temper."

Neither did I, Lane thought. He looked at MaryAnne.

"He's kind. He's angry. He and Jennifer would have arguments. She's as stubborn as he is. As far as I know it never got physical. I think he loved her." MaryAnne looked at the coffee machine.

Don got up to grab the pot and pour coffee for each of them. "Jennifer was mad at me after her last argument with him. She asked me what I thought of James, and I told her. She didn't like the answer." Don put the coffee pot back and sat down.

"What did you tell her?" Harper added sugar and milk to his coffee.

"The same thing I told you two about his temper. She said I should mind my own business, then she stopped talking to me." Don looked out the window when he heard a car drive by.

Looking to MaryAnne, Lane asked, "What was he angry about?"

"Being rejected by his family. They kicked him out right after high school. I think he's looking for a home. A family." MaryAnne lifted her coffee and took a sip.

"Do you know where we could find him?" Harper asked.

Don stood up and stepped into the front room so he could see out the front window. "He lives down in Bowness with a couple of other guys. They are all into motorcycles. Sometimes, they go racing in the summer." He grabbed a piece of paper and wrote on it. "Here's the address."

"He talked about visiting some friends out on the west coast once or twice." MaryAnne looked at the coffee inside her cup as if trying to read the future.

"She should never have hooked up with James." Don's head turned as a car drove by.

MaryAnne shook her head. "He is just a kid. I find it hard to believe that he would hurt Jennifer."

Lane and Harper left after assuring Jennifer's parents that they would provide them with daily updates.

Inside the Chevy, on their way down Shaganappi Trail, Harper asked, "How are Christine and Matt doing?"

Lane shrugged, remembering what he'd be up to on Saturday morning. "At each other's throats."

"Still?" Harper eased into the centre lane.

Lane nodded. "You bet."

"Think they'll ever get along?"

chapter 3

"What's going on?" Lane stepped over shoes scattered across the blue-grey linoleum inside their front door.

"Matt's invited some friends over." Arthur poked his head out from behind the hallway wall before disappearing back into the kitchen.

Lane stepped out of his shoes and followed Arthur. "How come you didn't tell me?"

"I found out an hour ago." Arthur reached into the fridge and pulled out a bottle of wine which he plopped on the kitchen table.

Music—Lane had never heard this kind before—rushed up the stairs from the family room, followed by a young man whose hair was almost as wild as the music. Lane readied himself for the inevitable curious gaze followed by an awkward conversation.

Instead, the boy stuck out his freckled hand. "I'm Fergus." A wide smile lit up the boy's face.

"Arthur." He wiped his hand on a tea towel before shaking hands with Fergus and smiling.

Fergus turned quickly before releasing Arthur's hand. "You must be Lane then. Matt brags that you're a detective." Fergus released Arthur's hand and reached for Lane's.

There's definitely an energy to this one, Lane thought. "Good to meet you, Fergus."

"Where's the can? The one downstairs is…" Fergus looked into the living room.

"Upstairs, to your right," Arthur said too quickly.

Fergus ran upstairs.

The doorbell rang.

Lane went to the door, where he found two young women and a male. At least Lane assumed it was a male. The trio had hair all of approximately the same length, all dyed black. *Their eclectic clothing is a delightful mix and match from the local secondhand store,* Lane thought.

"Is this Matt's place?" the male asked.

"Yes." Lane was relieved that he'd correctly guessed gender and opened the door.

"See, I knew where I was going," one of the females said as she stepped inside, kicked off her shoes, and followed the music down the stairs. The other two trailed her.

Lane looked to the bottom of the stairs. The three newcomers were embracing Matt.

"It's a party for the kids in the play. Matt said he invited a few over, word got around, and it ended up being a cast and crew party." Arthur set a bowl of salad on the table.

Lane fetched two plates and some cutlery. His mouth watered as he caught the scent of olives, cucumbers, tomatoes, oregano, peppers, onions, feta cheese, and vinegar. "Where did you get the tomatoes?"

"Lucked out at the Co-Op. Fresh ones just arrived when Matt and I were picking up a few things for the party." The doorbell rang again. "Maybe we should eat out on the deck. It's almost warm enough," Arthur said.

Matt hopped up the stairs. "Got it!" He looked to his left. "Hey uncle." Four young women were at the door. As they stepped in, one kissed Matt on the cheek.

Lane watched his nephew's neck turn red. The five trooped past, followed by Fergus. The girl who'd kissed Matt stopped at the top of the stairs. She wore a black floor-length dress. She stuck out a hand. "Carol."

After they'd made their way down the stairs, Lane leaned down to look into the family room. Someone had opened the sliding door. The party was spilling into the backyard. "How many are there?"

Arthur grabbed the salad bowl and wine. "Lots."

Lane followed with plates, forks, napkins, and glasses. "It's a good thing it warmed up so fast."

The deck was still heated by the afternoon sun, but a chill remained from the late-spring snowfall.

Lane loosened his tie and scooped salad onto their plates. Arthur poured the wine.

"How was today?" Arthur took a sip of wine.

"Chasing shadows. No sign of the missing woman or her boyfriend. Harper and I spent a day interviewing people at restaurants and bars in the area. Not one of them remembered seeing her." Lane guided the first forkful of salad into his mouth. He closed his eyes. "Delicious. Tomatoes that actually taste like tomatoes."

The back door opened. Christine stood framed in the doorway. She was wearing jeans and a white blouse. Her natural, graceful beauty struck Lane as he remembered holding her for the first time just moments after she was born.

She looked over her shoulder. "What's going on?"

"Matt decided the people in the play needed a get-together." Arthur settled a napkin onto his lap.

"Mind if I join you?" Christine asked.

"Not at all. Lots here. Bring a glass and plate." Arthur got up and brought another chair to the table.

Roz followed Christine when she stepped back out onto the deck. The dog curled up in a patch of sunshine while Christine put her purse on the deck and sat down with plate and cutlery. "You sure?" she asked again.

By way of reply, Lane took her plate and filled it with salad while Arthur poured her a glass of wine.

"How did class go today?" Arthur asked.

"Got an A on an English paper." She reached over, opened

her purse, pulled out the folded assignment, and handed it to Arthur.

Arthur began to read.

Lane raised his glass to Christine. "Congratulations." He smiled at the joy of an infrequent truce.

"It says you write with maturity, and that you've got definite talent," Arthur said as he handed the paper to Lane.

The back door opened. Fergus looked out. His eyes focused on Christine. He smiled, then disappeared back into the house.

"Who was that?" Christine asked.

"Fergus." Lane shook his head.

"What happened to your eye?" Christine asked.

"A tussle with a suspect," Lane said.

"A *tussle*?" Arthur's tone said he wasn't convinced even though Lane had phoned him shortly after the incident.

The door opened. Fergus stepped down onto the deck. He held one of Arthur's blown glass balls in his right hand. The colours in the glass glittered as Fergus made the ball roll along the back of his hand, then up his arm. Impossibly, the ball rolled over his shoulder, across the back of his neck and down to the fingertips of his left hand, where he balanced it before guiding it back the way it had come.

Arthur gasped when the ball fell from Fergus' shoulder, but the juggler recovered and caught the ball just centimetres from the deck's surface.

Lane and Arthur clapped. Fergus bowed and presented the ball to Christine. He closed the back door quietly behind him.

Christine began to eat her salad. She turned to Lane. "What time do you want to start tomorrow?"

You have no idea you've got an admirer, Lane thought.

chapter 4

"How about a rolo after we're done?" Lane asked Christine. They were walking along the alley running parallel to Kensington Road, where shops and restaurants lined either side of the street. Downtown high-rises and condos looked down on them from just across the river.

Christine wore jeans and a T-shirt. "What's a rolo?"

"Caramel, chocolate, espresso, and whipped cream." Lane looked to his right. They were crossing a street with a gate designed to reduce traffic into the residential area. The trees running down either side of the street, some with a hint of green buds, touched where they met above the middle of the pavement.

"What do these say?" Lane looked at a series of unique and stylized words sprayed on the side of a transformer.

"Not sure. There's another one of mine down there." Christine pointed at a green dumpster with one corner pushed up against a cinderblock building. She shook the green can of spray paint in her right hand.

"How many does that make?" Lane walked beside her.

"Nine or ten." Christine sprayed green over the stylized yellow letters of PARADISE and the red letters of HELL.

Lane looked down the alley. Another dumpster sat on a concrete pad next to a red brick wall. This time the container was navy blue. "Got the other can of paint?" Lane asked.

"In a minute."

Lane looked around him. Behind a store, further down the alleyway, a man sat on an upturned white plastic pail. The man stood, glared at Lane, flicked his smoke away, opened a door, and went inside.

Lane caught the scent of marijuana on the gentle breeze sliding through the alley. He walked closer to the dumpster. There was the sweet stink of something else in the air. It triggered memories of other times.

A garbage can.

A dead child.

A camper. Another dead child.

Lane's childhood, and a resurrected memory.

He looked on either side of the dumpster. The scent of death was stronger now. On the side of the container, he spotted a white message on the blue metal.

Lane looked around the alley for something to stand on.

"Uncle!"

Lane turned around.

Christine was only a few metres away. He read the anger in her eyes.

"I've been calling you!" She stopped with the can of paint hanging loosely at her side. "What's the matter?"

Lane pointed at the tag. "What's it say?"

Christine cocked her head to one side. "'Towers' I think, but the 'T' is kind of funky. So what?"

"It's the last name of the woman who went missing. Please, wait right there." Lane went up the alley and returned with the empty pail. He set it upside down next to the dumpster and stood on it.

"What's that smell?" Christine asked.

×

"What kind of lock set do you need?" The clerk wore a green canvas shirt that smelled of sawdust.

Maddy shifted her weight. The wooden floor creaked in protest. *This place is so last century*, she thought. "One to keep my bedroom door locked." The reply sounded sarcastic even to her. "Sorry."

The clerk lifted his cap and rubbed a bald spot stretching from forehead to crown. Dust fell from the cap. Particles were illuminated in a shaft of sunlight coming from the windows facing Tenth Street. "Safety an issue?"

Maddy nodded.

He picked a box off the shelf and handed it to her. "This one should do the trick."

"Do I need any tools?" Maddy cradled the box in the crook of her right arm.

"Got a Phillips?"

"What?" Maddy asked.

"Screwdriver. There'll be one over here." The clerk waved at her to follow him.

×

"How do you do this?" Christine wiped her nose with a wad of tissues. She stuffed them in her pocket then pulled them back out to compress them in her fist. "Do you think she was in there when I tagged the other dumpsters?"

Which question do I answer first? Lane thought. "I don't know if she was there or not. We'll have to wait until we get more facts."

"Well?" she wiped at her eyes.

"Well what?" Lane asked.

"How do you do this?" Christine watched him closely.

"Sometimes..." He searched his mind for the right words. She waited.

"Sometimes, it makes a difference."

"Who's he?" Christine pointed at an approaching man. He wore a white bunny suit and carried what appeared to be a toolbox.

"Dr. Colin Weaver." Lane watched Fibre approach.

She whispered, "Fibre?"

He nodded.

"He looks like a model."

Lane watched Christine's eyes as she studied the approaching Fibre. "Morning, Colin," Lane said.

Fibre appeared not to hear as he stopped and surveyed the scene. Police cruisers blocked both ends of the alley. The police forensics unit was parked about twenty metres away. Crime-scene tape formed a visible perimeter roughly ten metres out from the dumpster. "No one's been close to the scene?" Fibre asked in a voice free of emotion.

"Just me." Lane stood just outside the yellow tape.

"What's the pail doing there?" Dr. Weaver pointed at the white pail next to the dumpster.

"I put it there." Lane raised his cup in Fibre's direction.

Fibre sneered at Christine. "Who's this?"

"You're rude!" Christine stepped closer to Dr. Weaver.

Fibre looked down on Christine, even though they were approximately the same height. "What right does *she* have to be here?"

"She's a witness." Lane moved to separate them.

"You arrogant asshole!" Christine moved closer to Fibre.

Fibre ducked under the tape.

Lane looked around. Officers were moving closer, sensing trouble. He recognized one of them.

Fibre turned and threw a comment over his shoulder as he walked away. "Keep that mouthy bitch away from my crime scene." Then Fibre said, "Nigger."

Lane turned. At times like this, rage gave him a clarity of thought that he otherwise seldom experienced. "Fibre!"

Dr. Weaver turned.

Lane read anger and then shock in Fibre's eyes.

"She's my niece!" Lane measured the distance between himself and the doctor. The yellow tape was at Lane's chest. He lifted it with his right hand, preparing to duck under the tape while keeping his eyes on his prey.

Lane felt a hand grip the back of his belt.

"Detective. This isn't the place."

Lane swung around, wrenched himself free, and faced Sergeant Stephens. Her black, braided hair was dyed to hide the grey. Her green eyes locked on Lane's. Stephens smiled. "Long time no see."

Lane turned to look at Weaver. The doctor's face was white.

Rage made Lane mute.

"There are four other people who need a coffee. That makes seven including you and your niece." Stephens grabbed his arm and pulled him toward Christine. "Would you mind fetching us some while I speak with the good doctor?" Stephens asked.

"There's no way I'm fetching fucking coffee for that racist bastard!" Christine's voice shook with anger when she pointed at Dr. Weaver.

"This is a murder investigation. There's no way we're gonna have a brawl. Let me handle Weaver, and if you're not pleased with how I take care of the situation, then handle it your way *after* all the evidence is gathered. That way the scene is preserved, and we have a better chance of nailing whoever killed the girl." Stephens lifted her chin at Christine. "Fair?"

"Okay, but I'm not getting coffee for anybody," Christine said.

"Good. You've got a backbone. Every woman needs one." Stephens cocked her head in Lane's direction. "We'll let *him* get the coffee." She looked at Lane. "How come you haven't introduced me to your niece?"

"Kaye Stephens, this is Christine." Lane looked down at his shaking hands.

Kaye stuck her hand out, "Good to meet you, Christine." Christine smiled and shook the woman's hand.

Lane and Christine returned twenty minutes later. They leaned against a cruiser parked near the dumpster. Lane handed out the coffees. After that, they watched the dumpster. Every so often, the top of Fibre's bunny suit popped up before disappearing again.

"Sorry it took me so long to get here," Harper said as he approached Lane and Christine. "Where's my coffee?" he joked.

"Get your own fucking coffee," Christine said.

Lane glared at her.

"In Paradise I was always fetching coffee for the men. No more. Sorry Cam, the whole coffee thing is just…"

"Don't worry, I've already had enough coffee." Harper rubbed Christine's shoulder to say it was all good as far as he was concerned. "Besides, I have to ask you some questions since you were one of the first on the scene." He pulled out his hand-held computer.

Lane turned to watch the traffic across from the parking lot. Drivers slowed. Passengers touched their noses to side windows. A cyclist, wearing a reflective yellow vest with a red X, weaved between parked and moving cars. A crutch stuck out behind the seat of his bike, anchored to the crossbar of the frame. The cyclist was all muscle and sinew. He had his left hand on the bars. His right hand pushed down on his right knee each time it reached the top of the pedal's arc. The cyclist looked straight ahead without acknowledging the crime scene. *That's odd*, Lane thought.

Sergeant Stephens approached them. "Weaver's getting out of the dumpster. It's almost time to remove the body. The good doctor is coming over here. He's got something to say to you. Will you listen?" She aimed the question at Christine.

Christine nodded while sipping her coffee.

Stephens looked at Lane.

His shrug was noncommittal.

Stephens waited as Dr. Weaver climbed out of the dumpster, pulled off his rubber gloves, and walked over to the cruiser.

Christine set her coffee cup on the hood of a cruiser.

"Easy," Stephens said to Lane's niece.

"My outburst was regrettable. I apologize." Dr. Fibre pulled the hood of the bunny suit back so it rested around the back of his neck. His hair stuck to his scalp.

"Regrettable?" Christine asked.

Lane went to open his mouth only to find he couldn't form words. He studied Fibre, calculating an attack.

Weaver looked at Stephens, who glared back at him.

The doctor dropped his eyes, "Unacceptable."

"Unacceptable?" Christine blew steam with her hot coffee breath.

She's enjoying this, Lane thought.

"Totally unacceptable. I offer my apology," Fibre said.

"Lane?" Stephens asked.

"She's my niece." Lane put his coffee on the hood of the car.

Stephens moved to place herself between the doctor and the detective.

"Thus, making my comment all the more odious," Weaver said.

Lane thought he saw tears in the doctor's eyes.

The detective nodded.

"The body is ready for the Medical Examiner." Weaver said, and walked past them to the forensics unit vehicle.

Christine asked Stephens, "How did you get him to do that?"

"Told him he was getting a reputation for being a real chauvinist as far as the female officers were concerned, and that what he said to you was way over the line because it was racist as well. Then I said I'd be a witness if Lane wanted to file a report about the n-bomb. Thanks to you two, the opportunity finally presented itself for Fibre to get straightened out by a woman." Stephens put out her hand. "A real pleasure to meet you, Christine."

✕

"Where have you two been?" Arthur asked when they walked in the front door.

"We found the body," Lane said.

Christine went into the kitchen and downstairs into the family room. "Matt?" she called.

"Who found the body?" Arthur looked sideways at Lane.

"Christine and I found the body in a dumpster in the alley behind Kensington." Lane went into the dining room and grabbed his phone and ID. "Harper is on his way to pick me up. We have to break the news to the parents."

Lane went outside to wait for Harper and focus on the task at hand. He sat down on the front step.

A few minutes later, Arthur opened the aluminum door and looked down on him. "What happened besides discovering the body?"

Lane looked up. "Fibre dropped the n-bomb on Christine. If the sergeant hadn't stopped me... I was so angry. I would have..."

"Too bad you're missing it." Arthur looked down the street at the Chevy driving up the hill.

"Missing what?"

"The two of them are talking downstairs. Christine is explaining how you and the other officers stood up for her, and Matt is telling her how you've done the same for him. You're a hit with both of them." Arthur waved at Harper when he pulled up in front of the house.

"But…" Lane began.

"But nothing. Those two matter to us, and you make them feel like they matter. And, for what it's worth, whoever killed that girl, well, I wouldn't want to be them."

Lane looked up at Arthur. "What do you mean 'them'?"

"Sometimes you look right past the obvious. Dumpsters are pretty high. Christine says you had to stand on top of a pail to look inside. It would be pretty difficult for one person to put the body inside. And I almost pity the killers."

"Why's that?" Lane asked.

"Having Christine at the scene made this one personal. There's no way you'll back off until they're caught." Arthur closed the door.

Lane was quiet while Harper drove east on Crowchild Trail. Lane said, "Arthur thinks it would be difficult for one person to lift the body into the dumpster."

"He's right." Harper hesitated for a moment. "Stephens filled me in on what happened with Fibre. What he said to Christine was way out of line. How did you keep yourself from kicking his ass?" Harper asked.

"Sergeant Stephens stopped me." Lane looked ahead as they took the exit ramp and headed south.

"You okay to do this?" Harper turned right.

Lane looked at him. "I promised the parents I would keep them updated."

Inside the Towers' living room, Lane told Jennifer's parents,

MaryAnne and Don, about the discovery of the body and the necessity of having it identified.

"Was it quick?" MaryAnne asked. Her voice choked out the words. Her eyes were vacant, lost.

"It's too soon to know," Lane said.

"Was it that son of a bitch James?" The lines on Don's face seemed to deepen. His shoulders sloped forward, and his body sagged.

"Again, it's too early." Lane watched them get up in slow motion, and he thought, *It's amazing how two people can age ten years in less than a minute.*

chapter 5

"You haven't told me what you saw in the alley before you found the body." Harper sat across from Lane at a table outside of Kuldeep's coffee shop. Roz lay next to the table soaking up some of the morning sun.

"Where do you want me to start?" Lane looked at the mountains peaking out from behind the car dealerships lined up further down the street. Their peaks were still cloaked with white.

Roz poked Harper in the thigh with her nose. He rubbed her behind the ears. "You choose."

"Spent most of yesterday morning with Christine. She showed me how to read the graffiti. At first, I couldn't make any sense of the designs. It's like learning another language. By the time we got near the end, the message on that particular dumpster struck me as being out of place."

"In my mind, I'm still trying to decipher that message. I get the impression there's a whole bunch of information there, but I'm not sure what it is," Harper said.

"Or who put it there." Lane lifted his coffee cup and took a sip. "When I looked inside, the layer of newspapers, garbage bags, and paper towels was pretty deep. Still, the smell was strong, so I knew there was a body in there somewhere. After I pushed away some of the paper, I found her body tucked up against the near wall of the container. I think it was wrapped in clear plastic. It looked like the stuff you use to protect food before you put it in the fridge. And, the body was naked under the wrap."

"Any indication of the cause of death?" Harper asked.

"It could have been asphyxiation." Lane blinked quickly, hoping not to see a flashback of the dead girl's face. "Imagine where we'd be right now if the body had ended up in the landfill?"

"We'd be up to our knees in diapers. Now, what happened when Fibre arrived?" Harper stopped scratching Roz. She poked his hand with a cold nose.

"He treated Christine with contempt." Lane looked directly at Harper. "You know what he called her. That's when I started to go after him."

"And you're mad at yourself because you couldn't protect your niece from his bigotry. And you're mad at yourself for completely losing your cool." Harper's tone made it a statement of fact rather than an accusation.

Lane opened his mouth, closed it, then opened it again and said, "Yes."

"I have only one other question for now."

Lane waited.

"If you don't stick up for Christine, who will?"

Lane said, "Arthur told me much the same thing."

"And one other thing." Harper smiled.

"What's that?"

"How do I get Roz to leave me alone?" Harper laughed as the dog put her paws on the edge of the table and offered her puzzled expression to each of them in turn.

Lane shook his head and laughed. "She's got you now. You're helpless under her spell."

Harper pulled out his pocket computer. "Seems like we've got nothing but questions about this case."

"Where do we find James? That's question number one." Lane waved at Roz, and when she came close he rubbed her under her foreleg. She closed her eyes.

"Who painted the tag on the dumpster?" Harper's right hand tapped notes into his computer.

"Where are Jennifer's personal belongings?" Lane looked down at Roz. She turned her head to lick his hand.

"Why was Jennifer so upset when she came into the coffee shop?" Harper didn't look up.

"Was only one person involved in her death?"

"And what's with a dentist office where the appointment book is nearly empty and both dentists drive Mercedes?" Harper looked up at Lane.

"Maybe Ramona keeps appointments on the computer," Lane said.

"She referred to the appointment book when we asked about Jennifer's appointments."

"Maybe, when we get some answers, we'll have a better idea of who we're looking for." Lane stood up. "Coming over for breakfast?"

"Promised Erinn I'd help clean house. Ever since Jessica learned to walk, the house is a mess from the moment she gets up."

Lane stared at the mountains without really seeing them.

"What?" Harper asked.

"The anomalies. If past cases are any indication, the answers to the anomalies will lead us to the killer or killers." Lane turned to focus on Harper. "Somehow we have to find out who put the message on the dumpster. Why dump a body then advertise its location?"

×

"We have to go and get him stitched up." Arthur said, pointing to Fergus' foot which was wrapped in a towel.

Lane watched the scene unfold as he and Roz approached their house.

Fergus had one of his arms wrapped around Christine's shoulder as he hopped up to the open door of the Jeep and sat inside.

What did I walk into this time? Lane wondered as he spotted blood soaking through the white cotton towel covering the boy's foot. He also wondered if the smile on Fergus' face was from the pain or Christine's proximity. "I'll drive." He went to the gate and let Roz off her leash before getting her safely inside the yard. "Where's Matt?"

"Still asleep," Arthur said.

With Christine in the back seat propping up the white-faced Fergus and Arthur in the passenger seat, Lane started the engine. "Did you phone Fergus' parents?"

"They're in Mexico," Fergus said. "Please go to the Edgemont Clinic. I go there all the time."

Upon stepping through the door to the clinic, Lane discovered exactly what Fergus had meant. The nurse behind the desk surveyed the waiting fifteen or so patients, spotted Fergus' blood dripping on the linoleum, pushed a wheelchair their way and said, "Follow me, Fergus."

Lane and Christine sat side by side in the waiting room while Arthur went with Fergus, who threw a look of wounded longing Christine's way.

"What happened?" Lane asked.

"We were having coffee on the deck. Fergus decided we needed to see a juggling display. He used some of the knives from the kitchen," Christine said.

Lane shuddered at the vision of the carving knives stored in the wooden block by the kitchen sink.

"Everything was going fine until he decided he'd use four knives instead of three. The largest one got away from him and went right through his foot. Arthur had to pull the knife out, because it went about two centimetres into the wood and Fergus' foot was stuck to the deck." Christine looked to Lane when she finished the story. She furiously chewed her bottom lip.

Lane said, "What was Fergus doing on the deck so early on a Sunday morning?"

"He stayed over last night. Slept downstairs on the couch." Christine sat back and put her hands between her knees. She leaned to the left and rested her head on Lane's shoulder. Laughter poured out of her.

Five minutes later, after Lane managed to get Christine outside of the office, she choked out words between sobbing bouts of laughter. "The look on Fergus' face when the knife went into his foot. You know, he was so shocked, then he was stuck to the deck. I know it's not supposed to be funny, he was in so much pain, but it was hilarious!"

When Lane thought back on it, later — when there was time to look back — he realized this was the moment when Christine began to feel like part of their family.

chapter 6

"What would motivate someone to label the dumpster with Jennifer's name?" Harper turned the wheel and parallel parked between two cars in front of one of the coffee shops along Kensington Road.

"Or how would the person know where the body was? The killer wouldn't be sharing that information." Lane opened his door. "Maybe someone's onto the killer? Let's get a coffee first, then look around."

"First things first." Harper made no attempt to hide the sarcasm in his voice as he led the way up the stairs and into the coffee shop.

"Haven't seen you two in a while." Bryan greeted them from behind the espresso machine. His black hair was cut so short he could have moved south of the border and joined the Marines. "Nice eye, by the way."

Lane smiled and nodded.

"Thought we'd drop by for a visit. Got time to talk with us?" Harper asked.

"Let me start you with a couple of coffees first. One rolo and one black?" Bryan smiled at Lane.

"Good memory." Lane sat down at a table next to the window jutting out over the sidewalk running alongside Kensington Road. He looked out at the people walking along the street and the cars searching for a place to park.

"Bryan usually knows what's going on around here, so maybe he'll know where to find a graffiti artist or two." Harper sat down. His chair complained without surrendering to his weight.

"Who else besides the killers would know where the body was dropped? You'd think the plan would be to have Jennifer end up in the landfill and never be found," Lane said.

Bryan brought their coffees over. Lane's mouth watered when he saw the caramel crisscrossing the layer of whipped cream.

"So, how you guys been?" Bryan looked over his shoulder to see who was within earshot.

Lane took a sip and closed his eyes with pleasure. *Bryan is an artist,* he thought.

"We're looking for some help," Harper said.

"You heard about the body found in the back alley?" Lane asked and opened his eyes to study Bryan's reaction.

Bryan smiled, pretended to wipe the back of his hand across his lips, and handed Lane a napkin. "Yes."

Lane licked whipped cream and caramel from his top lip, took the napkin, and finished the job.

"We were wondering if you'd heard anything. We're looking for someone who's into graffiti." Harper set his coffee down.

Bryan looked out the window. He appeared to be studying the traffic.

Lane took in the room. People were drinking their coffees, eating, reading, talking, or working on laptops. No one was paying them any attention.

Bryan smiled. "Just a minute." He turned, walked alongside the counter, and into the kitchen.

Harper exhaled. "How come we always end up in a damned coffee shop?"

"Coffee's good. Great place to get information. Lots of people go for coffee, and they feel the need to talk. Graffiti artists are a closed community. This is as good a place as any to start finding out what we need to know." Lane sipped thought-fully. "My guess is you're going to need that computer."

Harper sighed and reached into the jacket pocket of his sports coat. He pulled out his palm-sized computer. "Ready."

The door to the kitchen pushed open. Bryan carried a couple of plates. As he worked his way toward the front of the shop, he dropped off the plates and picked up wooden spoons with numbers painted on them.

Bryan stopped at their table. "Malcolm. You look for a guy named Malcolm."

"That's all?" Harper asked.

"That's all he said. 'Tell them Malcolm is the guy to talk to.' The cook's pretty busy back there." Bryan looked around as a foursome climbed the steps and looked for an empty table.

"How come he gave us the name?" Lane asked.

Bryan smiled and leaned closer. "He's part of the Tran family. You guys have a good reputation with the family. Remember? The word is to help you two out when asked. The word comes from Uncle Tran himself."

"Oh." Lane sat back and thought, *I wonder how Uncle Tran's family is doing?*

"You kept your mouths shut, and you were fair. The family remembers stuff like that. The kids were taken care of and nobody came down on Uncle Tran. You guys did a good thing when you protected the kids first. Everyone in the family appreciated it. And Uncle Tran has one big family. Cheers." Bryan left.

"Malcolm?" Harper looked at Lane. "A first name. That's next to nothing to go on."

"Then let's start by checking out Mr. Sanders' address," Lane said.

×

He wiped black from his hands with a rag that had a patch or two of white on it. A tattooed dragon ran up his arm and inside his oil-stained T-shirt. His head was shaved; he stood as tall as Harper, and looked like he worked out. He stood in the shadow of an open overhead garage door. Lane saw that he was working on a motorcycle with a white number painted on the side. "Yes?" he asked as the detectives approached.

"We're looking for James Sanders." Harper stood in the sunlight, to Lane's right, just outside the garage. He reached inside his jacket.

"Don't worry, I don't need to see any ID. I'm Mike." He stepped outside. "Man, that sun feels good after the snow. Can't believe how quick it warmed up."

Lane looked inside the garage. There was a red toolbox on wheels, various motorcycle parts hanging from the wall, and more pieces sitting on the bench. "We need to talk with James."

"You the one he hit?" Mike pointed at Lane's bruised eye.

"Actually, he got both of us." Harper smiled and rubbed his ribs.

Lane thought, *This one is cagey, trying to show us how much he knows. Let him talk.* He waited.

"This is James' home address?" Harper looked over his shoulder as a car passed.

"He lives here. At least he used to. Haven't seen him since Thursday." Mike moved into the garage, scooped a pack of cigarettes off of the toolbox, and came back outside.

"And you know what happened to us." Lane laid it out like a fact.

"Of course." Mike struck a match and lit a smoke.

"We need to talk with him." Harper put his hands on his hips.

"You mean you want to arrest him." Mike took a deep pull on the cigarette, held it in his lungs, and blew smoke between the detectives.

Lane thought, *Time to cut to the chase.* "We need to establish if he had anything to do with Jennifer's death."

Mike pointed his cigarette at Lane and then Harper. "He wouldn't hurt her. He'd fight you two if he thought he had to, but he wouldn't hurt Jennifer."

"We still need to talk with him." Lane pulled out a business card and handed it to Mike.

Mike took the card and tucked in the back pocket of his jeans. He nodded. "Sure."

×

"I wonder when Roz will stop trying to pull my arm out of its socket?" Arthur wrapped the leash around his waist to take the pressure off his wrist, elbow, and shoulder. Roz wheezed harder.

"We're almost there. Want me to take her the rest of the way?" Lane looked at the sky. The sun was low in the west, but the remaining heat of the day made it possible for them to wear light jackets. "It's hard to believe it was snowing a couple of days ago." Lane looked for evidence of white under trees and in the lee of houses. There was none.

"Look at the buds." Arthur pointed at a tree. The tips of its branches were ripe with green.

"What's with Fergus?" Lane asked.

They crossed the road. Roz wheezed. Arthur let her off the leash. She bolted up the hill with her nose low and tail high.

"His parents are in Cancun for two weeks. He's looking after himself til they get back." Arthur rolled up the leash.

"So, he's living with us?" Lane asked.

Arthur looked at Lane. "I don't think so."

"That's good." Lane watched Roz digging in a tree well. "Why?"

"It's spring." Lane thought, *I hope I don't have to start drawing pictures for you.*

"What's that supposed to mean?"

"He's in love with Christine."

Arthur stopped. "What are you talking about?"

For once I'm the one who spotted the obvious, Lane thought. "He's always showing off for her. Not a whimper out of him when he puts a knife through his foot. Smiles all the way to the clinic while she has her arm around him in the back seat of the Jeep."

"Oh my God! He can't live with us!" Arthur looked for Roz. "We have to send him home!"

"Relax." Lane wasn't sure if he should laugh or be alarmed.

"Christine's very vulnerable right now! Roz! Come Roz!" Arthur waved at the dog. She lifted her head, then went back to digging. Arthur rushed toward her.

"You don't think they've been up to something, do you?" Lane asked, finding himself on the same panicked wavelength as Arthur.

"Fergus needs to get back into his own house! We've got to get him away from her." Arthur whistled at the dog.

"If we get rid of him, won't that make him all the more attractive to Christine?"

×

"I'll give you a ride home, Fergus, right after supper." Arthur handed over a plate of Greek salad with half a loaf of French bread.

"Thanks." Fergus grabbed the plate with his left hand and continued to channel surf with his right.

Arthur left the family room and went back to the main floor. "He eats fast. I'll go start the Jeep. You bring him out." He grabbed his keys and coat, stuffed his feet in his shoes, and proceeded out the front door.

Lane looked at Roz, who lay on the floor with her chin

resting on her front paws. She raised her eyebrows at him.

A belch rumbled up the stairs.

"Finished?" Lane called to Fergus.

"Yep."

Lane went down to the family room and steadied Fergus as he hopped up the stairs. "Thanks for giving me a ride home."

Lane watched the steps. "No problem. It's not like you could walk."

"And the food's great here. That salad was…" Fergus was lost for words.

Lane guided him outside and into the front seat of the Jeep.

"I'm buying some new practice knives tomorrow. And some steel-toed boots." Fergus smiled as he put on his seat belt.

"See you, Fergus." Lane shut the door.

Arthur eased the Jeep down the driveway.

Lane watched until they turned the corner at the end of the block.

The phone was ringing when he went inside. He checked the caller ID and picked up the phone. "What's up?"

Harper said. "Jennifer Towers' funeral is tomorrow. Just got the call. Interment is at Queen's Park Cemetery."

"We'd better be there in case Mr. Sanders shows. What time?"

"Ten in the morning. I'll pick you up at seven." Harper hung up.

Fifteen minutes later, Lane heard Christine walk in the front door. "Where's my baby? Where's my puppy?" she asked.

In the family room, Lane watched Roz hide behind the couch with head and tail held low. "We're down here," he said. Lane could hear Christine drop her purse, shoes, and jacket at the front door.

Christine came down the stairs to where Lane sat reading a book.

"Where's Fergus?" she asked.

"He went home." Lane put the book down and waited for a reaction.

"Good." She sat down in the chair and swiveled so that she was facing him. "Where's Roz?"

Lane said, "Good?"

"I thought he was gonna move in." Christine crossed her legs and tucked them under her thighs. "Look, I know you think I'm crazy because of Paradise and everything. And sometimes when I think about it, when I think about what they did to me, I get angry. But that doesn't mean I'm interested in Fergus just 'cuz he's interested in me."

Lane closed his mouth and thought, *Now she's reading my mind!*

"He needs someone to look out for him, that's all. So I'm gonna ask Matt to invite him over again. Fergus needs people around." Christine cocked her head to one side, waiting.

"What do you want to do about your father?" Lane felt tightness in his chest. He reached up and tried to rub it away.

"I want to go and see him. I checked it out. He's supposed to be coming to town. I don't need to meet him, just see him. Maybe it'll…" Christine's voice was choked off.

"Do you want me to go with you?"

"Would you?" she asked.

×

"Maddy?" Andrea's voice was a little angry.

She's overtired, Maddy thought. "Yes?"

"Where you go at night?" Andrea rolled over so she could see Maddy better.

"How did you know that?" She turned and watched Andrea's expression.

She looked at Maddy with those overlarge eyes. Andrea wore white and red pajamas. Her blonde hair was cut short. "Because."

"Don't worry. You're safe. I'm the only one with a key to the door. Besides, I'm never far away."

chapter 7

"Any idea why he wants to see us?" Lane watched the C-train rumble across a downtown intersection. The rails bobbed as the wheels traveled over a soft spot. A pedestrian ran across the tracks just in front of the train.

Harper shook his head. "People always want to beat that damned train. As far as us visiting Smoke, I have no idea why he called us. I'm totally out of the loop when it comes to the whys and hows of the new top cop. You do know who Chief Smoke's new assistant is?" The light turned green.

Lane looked at Harper's face. There was no hint of a smile. Lane waited.

"Stockwell." Harper gave his head a disgusted shake and turned left into a parking lot fenced in by chain link. The detectives' chins dipped as the car bounced over a speed bump.

Five minutes later, they found themselves sitting across from Stockwell, who sat behind a semicircle of a desk that took up more than half of the space in the waiting room. He'd greeted them with a nod as he typed on the keyboard beneath a top-of-the-line computer screen. There was a black earpiece and threadlike microphone attached to the right side of his face.

Lane took in the room. *Everything about this place screams change.* He looked at Harper, who was frowning.

"Chief'll see you now." Stockwell, with trimmed eyebrows and gelled hair, didn't look up from behind his designer glasses.

Harper launched himself from his chair. Lane followed.

The inside of the chief's office seemed bigger somehow.

Pictures of the new chief and various current city celebrities were carefully aligned along one of the oak walls.

Smoke's six-foot frame was swallowed by a high-backed black leather chair behind a bird's-eye maple desk. The desk dwarfed a computer screen even larger than Stockwell's. Smoke's back was to the window overlooking the downtown. He glanced at the reflection of his gold braid in the mirror-like polish of the speckled wood.

Lane squinted as he tried to read the features of Smoke's face, which were overexposed by the glare of the day's intense sunshine.

Smoke stood. Leather sighed. He reached across the desk to shake their hands. Lane felt Smoke's limp grip and noticed his manicured fingernails.

Smoke sat down first. "Please sit down, detectives."

Lane and Harper sat in the oak chairs arranged across the no man's land of Smoke's desk.

"It's a new policy of mine to check with detectives and stay abreast of investigations. The high profile of your last two cases encourages me to initiate a proactive approach." Smoke leaned back in his chair.

What new policy? Lane looked at Harper to see if he'd heard of the new policy.

Harper's puzzled expression was enough of an answer.

"It's an integral and key component of my new and innovative approach to law enforcement," the chief said.

Lane looked beyond Harper to a photo on the wall. Smoke, Bishop Paul, and Dr. Jones posed with raised crystal glasses of amber. They smiled with self-assured superiority as they looked up from a table. A waiter stood behind them holding a bottle of scotch that Lane would have guessed to be a quarter of a century old.

Smoke moved from behind his desk to stand between Lane and the photograph.

Lane focused on the chief's smile. *It's the same one he gave me when the officers were beating the hell out of that guy on the dirt bike.*

"How are you progressing on the Towers case?" Smoke asked.

Lane felt Harper's eyes on him.

Lane said, "Initial indications are that the boyfriend may be a person of interest." He sensed Harper struggling to maintain his composure.

"That's very good news!" Smoke slapped his hand on the desk. He moved closer and stood over Lane, who caught a sweet shock wave of alcohol, aftershave, and mouthwash. "I'll expect an update if there are any new developments. You can depend on my full support."

Sensing they were being dismissed, Lane and Harper stood.

"Would you like a daily or weekly update, sir?" Harper asked.

"Weekly will suffice." Smoke's tone had changed. He obviously had more important matters to deal with.

Lane and Harper stepped into the waiting area. Stockwell remained focused on his monitor. Lane spotted a game of solitaire on the screen just before it changed to an official-looking document with the city's coat of arms on top.

The detectives maintained their silence in the elevator where they, along with other officers and city workers, were whisked down to street level.

They stepped outside the controlled air of the building and walked to the unmarked Chev.

They were driving out of the downtown core before either spoke.

"If this is a new and improved approach to policing, why does Dr. Jones belong to Smoke's old boys' network?" Lane asked.

"And why is Stockwell Smoke's right hand man?" Harper asked.

"The other question is why is the chief using aftershave and mouthwash to hide the smell of booze?"

"You smelled it too?" Harper asked.

Lane nodded. He remembered McTavish's voice when he'd said, "Watch your back."

×

"This has to be the worst part of the job," Harper turned right and followed a procession of vehicles into Queen's Park Cemetery. Evergreen trees lined either side of the road.

Lane thought back to another case. *I wonder if Randy still works here?*

"Remembering our first case?" Harper asked.

Now, he's reading my mind! Lane thought. "I wonder if we'll bump into Randy?"

Harper looked to the left, then looked ahead as they trailed the procession of limousines and a somber parade of other vehicles. "All of the other unmarked units are waiting at the exits. They have a description of Mr. Sanders."

"I'm not sure I want him to show up." Lane looked across the valley as they started down the slope. Many of the trees had a haze of green in their branches from buds waiting to erupt. The evergreens wore a coat of winter dust and pollution as they waited for the spring rain.

"What do you mean?"

"He'll probably run. Chases usually end badly." Lane saw the hearse stop near a mound of earth. The trailing drivers stopped in a line behind it.

Harper turned left at the bottom of the hill, then made a quick U-turn. "Now we're ready if we have to leave in a hurry."

Lane grabbed the Nikon binoculars. Harper took the digital

camera with the long lens. They took up positions where they could get a clear look at the mourners gathered around the grave.

Lane heard the shutter of Harper's camera as he began to pick his targets. They worked methodically though the mourners listening to the minister.

"You guys must love hangin' around here. Kind of expected you to show up this morning."

Lane looked to his left as he worked his way around the rotund tree trunk. "Hello, Randy." *He hasn't changed much. Yet, there's something quite different about him.*

"It's been a year or two." Randy took his green hard hat off and used the inside of his elbow to wipe the sweat from his forehead.

"Haven't changed your wardrobe, I see." Lane smiled.

Randy looked down at his green nylon jacket and green cotton work clothes. "Not a lot of imagination around here when it comes to style."

Lane chuckled. "How are Ernie and Beth doing?"

Randy's face turned red.

Oh, I never saw that one coming. Randy and Beth are an item now, Lane thought. "We're looking for a suspect. He's a little under six feet, barrel-chested, powerfully built, blond hair."

"That's where you got the eyeshadow?" Randy asked.

It was Lane's turn to blush at the memory of James leaving the bruise under Lane's eye. *Same old Randy putting me on the defensive,* he thought.

"That's what I thought. Is there anyone covering over there?" Randy pointed north along the pathway that exited at the northeast corner of the cemetery. "The one you're looking for has dyed his hair black. He parked his motorcycle next to the fence."

"Thanks." Lane waved to get Harper's attention.

"No, I've been meaning to thank you. Ernie and Beth are thriving." Randy threw the comment over his shoulder as he walked away.

Harper turned in Lane's direction. He pointed in the direction of the crowd dispersing from the gravesite. One of the mourners was walking north. He wore black jeans and a black leather jacket. He ducked behind a gravestone, then re-appeared with a black helmet that he promptly put on before adjusting the chinstrap.

Lane began to follow. He could hear Harper talking into his radio, "The suspect is headed northeast along the pathway."

The man in black looked over his shoulder, spotted Lane and Harper, and broke into a run.

Lane tucked the binoculars in the crook of his arm and gave chase. The May breeze licked his face and bit at his lungs.

The suspect ducked in behind an evergreen tree next to the chain link fence.

The wind carried the wail of approaching sirens.

Lane was twenty metres away from Sanders when he heard a starter whine and the motorcycle engine rev. The bike shot out from behind the tree and skidded on a patch of grass. The rear tire chirped as it hit the paved pathway. The rider opened the throttle, balanced on the rear wheel, and threaded his way through the opening in the fence. He dropped the bike back down onto both wheels and turned right.

Lane ran past the trees, down the path, and out onto the sidewalk. He looked at the intersection. The traffic light was yellow. The motorcycle accelerated. A police cruiser was closing in. An oncoming car turned left in front of the motorcycle.

Smoke boiled around the rear tire of the motorcycle as the rider braked. The back end of the bike twisted to catch up to the front. When the motorcycle slammed into the rear fender of the car, the rider was launched over the trunk. He skidded across the intersection on his chin, rolled onto his back, and lay still.

Lane looked around the intersection. An eastbound cruiser braked and blocked traffic. Another skidded on a patch of gravel, creating a cloud of dust that swept across the intersection. Lane ran into the cloud and found the rider trying to get up. The rider rolled, sat down, and took off his helmet. James Sanders looked up at Lane.

Lane stood over him. They were momentarily alone inside the dust cloud. James wiped the back of his hand across his face. Dirt mixed with tears and left streaks of mud across his face.

Lane pulled out a pair of handcuffs.

"I think I broke my leg." James held out his hands.

Lane looked at the pale face and the leg bent at an unnatural angle below the knee.

Lane put the cuffs away.

An officer approached with his hand on his revolver. "Need an ambulance?"

James began to shiver.

Lane nodded. "And a blanket."

×

"We need to be there when he's in recovery." Lane paced the floor in the waiting room of the Foothills Medical Centre emergency room.

"Look, I'm going to get a coffee. You want one?" Harper reached into his pocket for money.

Lane nodded. "I'm staying here. We can't miss this chance." He watched the clock and then the TV in the corner. Patients ambled in, the automatic doors opened and closed, a woman snored in a chair, and Lane paced.

Harper returned. "Here." He offered Lane a coffee.

"Thanks." Lane took his and sipped. He closed his eyes. *Maybe the coffee will help,* he thought.

"Talk," Harper said.

Lane turned to his partner. Harper guided him over to a pair of chairs set apart from the others in the waiting room.

"What do you mean?" Lane asked.

"Look, you don't get like this unless you're on someone's trail or your world is turning upside down. So talk." Harper leaned back, crossed his ankles, and waited.

"Christine's father is coming to town, and she wants me to take her to see him." *Why was that the first thing that came out of my mouth?* Lane wondered.

"You're worried about losing her?"

"Or her getting hurt. I mean my sister has already abandoned Christine. Her father hasn't ever wanted to have anything to do with her. In fact, he's denied being her father." Lane looked at the wall.

"It's out of your hands, then?"

Lane thought for a minute. "I guess so."

"Just like this case?" Harper turned as a nurse stepped out of emergency to scan the crowd.

"None of it makes sense. It would take two normal-sized people to put the body in the dumpster. I have no idea how Sanders could transport a body on a motorcycle. People keep vouching for James. I pick up really weird vibes from the dentist. Yet, why would the car be left outside of the dentists' office? It's so obvious. The killer can't be that stupid. And then there's the tag on the dumpster. What kind of killer would advertise where the body was dumped? Absolutely nothing adds up."

The nurse walked over to Lane and Harper. "I was asked to let you know that James Sanders is on his way to recovery. You wanted to talk with him. The surgeon had to put a rod in his leg. The tibia was broken in several places. So you need to keep the visit short."

Within five minutes they were outfitted in masks and gowns designed to fit everyone and no one.

James was on a gurney. There was one other patient in the room. The stink of disinfectant, vomit, and blood was in the air.

Harper asked, "We're not going to use this testimony, right?"

Lane watched the suspect. "Of course not, but we may at least find out where to look after this. It's pretty difficult to lie when you wake up from anesthetic."

James' eyes began to open.

Lane pulled a couple of chairs over beside the gurney so they could sit eye-to-eye with James. Harper sat down next to Lane.

"James?" Harper asked.

James' eyelids took at least ten seconds to open. He licked his lips. His eyes appeared unfocused. "I'm gonna be sick."

Lane looked around, spotted a kidney-shaped green plastic bowl, and reached for it. He put it against James' cheek. Sanders lifted his head and heaved. Harper found a tissue to wipe mucous from the boy's mouth.

"Thanks," James said.

Lane set the bowl next to a nearby sink.

Harper said, "We've got some questions."

"Did they cut off my leg?" James asked.

"They put a rod in it." Harper waited for Lane to sit back down.

"Oh." James looked at each of them. "Sorry about the eye, man."

"What were you and Jennifer fighting about?" Lane asked.

"Asshole." James lifted his arm from under the blanket.

"What?" Lane asked.

"I called her father an asshole. She got mad at me. We were supposed to meet at the sports bar after work that day. I waited. She never showed." It sounded like he had meatballs in his mouth. His speech was barely coherent.

"When did you talk with her last?" Harper asked.

"Night before that. On the phone. I apologized. We were gonna meet and have a bite. Talk. I loved her, man." James' voice got rough. He cleared his throat.

"Who killed her?" Lane asked.

James' tone was flat. "Don't know, man. Don't know. I loved her, man. You didn't know her. She was determined. Alive. Smart. Who could kill somebody like that?" James began to weep.

✕

"Who's here?" Lane stepped inside the front door. He used his foot to push aside a factory-outlet shoe-store selection of footwear scattered just inside the doorway.

"Matt, Christine, Fergus, and some friends. By the way, there's one beer and a frosted glass in the fridge for you." Arthur sat on the tan leather couch in the living room. He saluted Lane with a glass of beer.

Lane took off his jacket and hung it on the back of a kitchen chair.

"How did things go at the hospital? Have you caught the killer?" Arthur put one foot on the coffee table.

"I don't think so. His leg is badly broken. He'll be in the hospital for a week or so. We interviewed him right after he came out of the anesthetic. I don't think he did it. And there are still too many unanswered questions." Lane reached into the freezer for the glass and into the fridge for the beer. He opened the bottle.

They heard a clang.

"What was that?" Lane asked.

"Fergus is practicing out on the deck."

Lane opened the back door. Fergus looked up as he picked up a knife from beside the barbecue. He was wearing a helmet, heavy work boots, and safety glasses.

Roz looked out from under the safety of the table.

Christine sat in the corner on the other side of the deck. "Don't worry, uncle, the knives are for practice. They're dull."

Fergus stood up and balanced on his good foot. "Arthur said I had to wear all this stuff if I was going to practice out here."

Lane poured his beer. On a whim he asked, "Either of you heard of a graffiti artist named Malcolm?"

Fergus and Christine looked at one another.

Lane thought, *They know the name!* He forced himself to concentrate on pouring the beer, and was satisfied with the lack of foam.

Fergus threw one knife in the air, then added a second and a third.

Lane stood transfixed by the glitter of the sun off metal. The knives rose and tumbled in their dance.

"Why do you want to know?" Christine watched her uncle watch the knives.

"It's part of the investigation Harper and I are working on." Lane sipped the beer, smiled, and kept his eyes on Fergus.

"How did you know I was into graffiti?" Fergus was getting out of sync.

"I didn't. We were told to look for a guy named Malcolm, so I thought I'd ask the two of you," Lane said.

Fergus caught one knife, a second, and the third clanged off the barbecue. It hit the deck and skittered under the table.

Roz moved sideways to be closer to Christine. "Enough practicing," Christine said.

Fergus crawled under the table to retrieve his knife.

"So, you know about Malcolm, but you're not going to tell the police." Lane sat on the back step.

"It's just that…" Fergus began.

"Graffiti artists don't talk to the police. That's just the way it is," Christine said.

"So, how do I find Malcolm?" Lane sipped his beer and waited.

Fergus looked to Christine.

Roz put her head on her paws and looked at Lane.

"Try the phone book," Fergus said.

Lane ate alone after Arthur left to drive Fergus home. Christine, Matt, and Carol, who was becoming a regular visitor, watched a movie.

Lane savoured the salmon. Arthur had baked it with honey, lemon, ginger, and sesame oil. He glanced at the phone in the corner of the living room by the grandfather clock. He stood up, went to the clock, and bent down to pick up the phone book. Lane flipped through the directory, sipped his beer, and took another bite of salmon. He found Malcolm's Custom Body Works in bold black letters. Lane read the address and saw that it was just off Centre Street.

chapter 8

"This is a long shot." Harper turned off of Centre Street, headed down the hill, and approached Edmonton Trail. Shops, small industries, and a hardware and building supplies store thrived where a drive-in theatre used to exist.

"He said look in the phone book. The name kind of jumps out at you." Lane checked the addresses. "Must be a couple of blocks over." He pointed to the right.

Harper turned at the lights.

They found Malcolm's Custom Body Works sandwiched between an automotive-supply shop and a paper-recycling depot. Vintage car bodies, frames, and engines were arranged in neat rows in front and alongside the south wall of the shop. Some of the cars wore fresh coats of paint, while others were cloaked with rust.

Harper parked off to one side of a ramp leading to the open mouth of an overhead door. The inside of the shop was hidden in shadow. The whine of tools, powered by compressed air, carried out into the yard. Lane got out of the passenger door and strode up the ramp. Harper followed.

Inside, their eyes adjusted to the artificial light. They saw car bodies being prepped for paint. The centrepiece was a 1953 Ford pickup truck, customized and lowered to the point where it looked futuristic rather than antique. Its candy-apple red finish glowed from countless coats of clear finish.

A man poked his clean-shaven head from behind the fender of the Ford. He lifted his safety glasses and focused on the detectives. Lane watched as other pairs of eyes spotted the officers. Then, deciding there wasn't enough to hold their interest, the workers continued on with their tasks.

"Over here!"

Lane and Harper turned toward the voice coming from their right. The man was at least six feet tall, weighed over two hundred pounds, and wore blue coveralls and a ball cap. He motioned for the detectives to come into the front office.

Lane closed the door behind them so that normal conversation would be possible.

"What's up?" the man asked as he sat in a red office chair that was remarkably free of dirt.

Lane and Harper sat down on either side of a blue water cooler.

A blonde woman turned around in her chair to study the detectives. Lane noted her blue eyes appraising him at the same time he studied her.

She's about the same age as him: twenty-five to thirty, Lane thought.

Harper pulled a folded image from his pocket. It was a photograph of the dumpster where Jennifer Tower's body was discovered. "We're looking for Malcolm."

"You found him." Malcolm leaned forward in his chair.

He's trying to sound nonchalant, but it's not working. Lane observed the intensity of Malcolm's eyes and the way his posture changed.

"Could you help us identify the person who created this?" Harper handed the tag to Malcolm.

Malcolm took the paper. He carefully placed it on the desk and traced the letters with the pinky finger of his right hand. He looked up. "Okay."

Lane said, "We'd like to find the artist. Can you help us?"

Malcolm handed the picture back to Harper.

"Well?" Harper asked.

"Pretty graphic." Malcolm leaned back. "Have you met

Harry?" He nodded at the woman behind the other desk.

Harry stood, walked around the desk, and shook hands with each of the detectives. "Charmed." She smiled to ease the sarcasm in her voice.

Lane thought, *There's no way we're going to be able to force either of these people to do what they don't want to do.* "What do you mean?" Lane asked Malcolm.

"Sorry?" Malcolm tilted his head to one side.

"You said it was pretty graphic." Lane stood up, took the picture from Harper, and handed it back to Malcolm.

Malcolm leaned forward to set the tag on his desk. "See here. The way the 'W' and the 'O' are drawn." He pointed at the letters.

Lane leaned forward to take a closer look.

"More than a suggestion of something sexual there. And, by the placement of the letters and the arrow, I'd say it's gender specific." Malcolm looked at Lane.

"You're saying it's sexual?" Lane asked.

"It's certainly open to that interpretation." Malcolm nodded his head toward Harry, indicating that she should take a look.

Lane moved to his left. Harry stood between Lane and Malcolm. Harper joined them.

"Crotch shot," Harry said.

"What would be the point of that kind of message?" Harper asked.

"Don't know," Malcolm said.

"But it's definitely there," Harry said.

"Are you in the habit of finishing each other's sentences?" Lane smiled.

"Yes," Malcolm said.

"All the time," Harry said.

"How come you know so much about graffiti art?" Lane asked.

"I was into it for a few years. It's how Harry and I met." Malcolm leaned back in his chair.

"Whose is this?" Harper pointed at the photo.

"Not sure," Malcolm said.

"But you have an idea," Lane said.

Malcolm nodded.

"It may help us solve a murder." Harper stepped back.

"The girl in the dumpster?" Harry asked.

Malcolm made eye contact with Harry.

"She was an only child. The wall in her parents' house is covered with landmarks of her life," Harper said.

A hit! Lane thought. *Harper, you've got them!*

Malcolm looked at Harry. She lifted her chin. Her eyes filled with tears.

Malcolm held out his hand. "You got a card? I'll ask around. You might start by talking with Leo. He knows the area."

"Leo?" Lane asked.

"Don't know his last name," Harry said.

"He's been in the Kensington area for more than ten years," Malcolm said. "Kind of an institution."

"How will we recognize this Leo?" Harper asked.

Malcolm looked at Harry. They both laughed. "Can't miss him," Harry said.

×

"What now?" Lane asked.

"McTavish just called. He wants us to meet him in Kensington." Harper waited for Lane to close the car door.

Lane handed Harper a coffee. "What does he have?"

"Another message on a dumpster. Says we need to see it." Harper waited for Lane to buckle up, put on his signal light, and turned west onto 20th Avenue and south at the elementary school.

Lane thought, *How come we're always playing catch-up?*

"What are you thinking?" Harper drove under the LRT bridge and past Riley Park.

"We've got to get a jump on this case instead of always trying to catch up. It looks like there's only one way to do that."

"What's that?" Harper asked.

"You're not going to like it."

Harper turned west onto Kensington, then left down a back alley. A blue and white cruiser was parked in front of a blue dumpster at the back of Pages Books. McTavish had finished taping off the alleyway to traffic. He waited while Lane and Harper parked and exited their vehicle.

"Think there's something here for you." McTavish pointed to his left at the blue dumpster which sat up against a fence faded grey by wind, rain, sun, and winter. Lane spotted the image, then ducked under the tape, being careful where he put his feet. He stood about a metre away from the dumpster. Most of the image was in red. The name "Towers" was wrapped in a web. A spider approached, ready to devour the name wrapped in nearly transparent white silk. Lane looked closely at the spider's eyes. They were composed of pairs of ones and zeroes.

Harper had the digital camera in his hand and began to snap shots from a variety of angles.

"What do you make of the eyes?" Lane asked.

"No idea," McTavish said.

Harper shrugged. "Binary?"

"What?" Lane looked closer at the spider.

"You know, a series of ones and zeroes. Computer language." Harper looked at the back of the digital camera to check the images.

Lane walked around one side and then the other. He looked for something to stand on.

"I already checked inside. It's empty." McTavish picked up a four-litre paint can he'd found across the alley. "Take a look if you like."

Lane thought, *We get more questions than answers from the person who is doing these tags.* "I'll wait for forensics," he said.

Ninety-five minutes later, Lane, Harper, and McTavish went around the corner and across the street to the coffee shop.

"Bryan's probably in the back," Harper said as Lane ordered and McTavish found them a table.

"You two always this upscale?" McTavish asked.

"What do you mean?" Harper asked.

Lane looked at the young woman operating the espresso machine while he listened to McTavish and Harper.

"I mean you pay twice what I pay for a cup of coffee." McTavish smiled.

"We like to get to know the people who run the coffee shops. It gets to be like a pipeline." Harper looked to see if Lane was going to jump in.

You're doing just fine, Lane thought.

"Oh." McTavish didn't look convinced.

"Like the other day…" Harper looked at Lane. "Kuldeep."

"What?" McTavish leaned back as their coffees arrived. His leather belt creaked.

Harper asked, "Bryan around?"

The young woman in black answered, "I'll get him for you."

Lane smiled at the thought of the first sip of coffee.

"Junkie," McTavish smiled.

Lane and Harper looked at him.

"You're hooked on this stuff." McTavish lifted his cup in a toast to caffeine.

Lane took his first sip, put the cup down, and smacked his lips. He gave Harper a sideways glance. "You were saying?"

"How come Kuldeep won't go to the dentist next door?" Harper asked.

"Good question," Lane said.

"Who's the dentist?" McTavish asked.

"Rockwell Sedation Dentistry." Harper lifted his coffee.

"Let me check, but I think I heard something about that place. Two dentists, right?" McTavish looked at the wall beside the fireplace, trying to remember.

"That's right." Harper pulled the palm-sized computer from his pocket.

"The price of coffee's getting to look more and more like a bargain when it comes to information," McTavish said.

And I was beginning to think we were at a dead end, Lane thought.

Bryan stepped up to the table, wiping his hand with a dishtowel and sporting a new diamond stud in his left nostril. "What's up?" He looked around the table and skipped over McTavish.

"He's okay," Lane said.

"Just never met him before," Bryan said.

"I trust him," Harper said.

Bryan shrugged as if to say, "I'll make up my own mind."

"We're looking for a graffiti artist named Leo." Lane looked over the rim of his cup as he sipped.

Bryan shook his head. "You don't know what you're asking."

"What are we asking?" Harper glanced across the table at Lane.

"Leo's kind of a hero around here. Remember when the premier got drunk and went after those homeless people down at the shelter? Leo made it news while the local papers kept the story on the back pages. Leo talked with the homeless guys who sell papers on the street. Got the story from them. Leo's version turned out to be more accurate than the ones on TV and in the newspapers. Leo painted tags and political cartoons on the windows of different shops, including this one. Got lots of people talking about the homeless and what an arrogant ass the premier was. Some of the business owners got upset. Some forgot about it after the rain washed away Leo's stuff. He uses water-soluble paints." Bryan turned to McTavish. "Some of the businesses got the police out to go after the graffiti artists. All I know is that whenever Leo comes in here for a coffee, he never gets the money for it out of his own pocket. Someone always pays for his coffee. If I told you how to find Leo," Bryan looked around at the patrons who were quietly listening in, "I'd lose most of my customers."

×

"Saturday night?" Lane sat in the front room in an easy chair. He reached for the beer on the coffee table.

"You said you'd come. Matt's coming too. So's Uncle Arthur." Christine plopped onto the couch and tucked her legs up under her backside.

Lane watched Christine closely. *I wonder if she'll ever figure out how beautiful she is?* he thought.

"Well?" Christine's voice was like steam in a kettle — evidence of something below the surface ready to boil over.

Lane kept his voice low and soft in an attempt to prevent that from happening. "Of course I'll go with you. Maybe we should go out for dinner as well. Where is this going to happen?"

Christine glared at him.

She just wants to fight with someone, anyone. She's stressed, and a fight would be a release, he thought.

"The Red and White Club." She dropped the words like a challenge.

"At the stadium?" Lane realized he'd allowed a bit of surprise to creep into his voice.

"So? What's the problem?" Christine seemed to be tensing the muscles in her arms and back.

"No problem." *Are you kidding? Isn't it obvious why I wouldn't want to go there? That place is a bastion for macho sportsmen and I'm very far from being one of them,* he thought.

"I can tell you want to say something. You think I shouldn't do this, don't you?" Christine sagged into the couch.

"I'm worried."

"About what?" Christine waited for the bad news.

"About you getting hurt if you do go. And, if you don't go to see him, you'll always wonder. I understand that you need to go. You already know all of this! It's why you're so stressed." Lane reached for his beer and took a sip. *Maybe this will shut me up!*

"Shit." Christine closed her eyes. "I can't sleep. I can't stop thinking about it and how it will turn out."

Lane nodded.

"It's my father. You know?"

Yes I do know. That's the problem. My father gave up on me a long time ago, he thought.

"You'll be there, right?"

Lane nodded. "I will. And we'll go for dinner. There's a great Vietnamese restaurant I've been wanting to take you to."

chapter 9

Football Looks to Past Heroes

Flagging ticket sales have encouraged Stampeders management to call on famous players from the past. Bobbie 'Go Long' Green will be the featured speaker at the Red and White Club.

This Saturday-night event will celebrate Green's stellar season as a wide receiver before he went south for a record-setting career in the NFL.

chapter 10

"Maddy?"

She turned around in the empty high-school hallway as she passed the front door of the office. "Mr. Herrence." She took in his fifty-year-old paunch and his black pompadour, wondering, not for the first time, if his hair was real.

"I've been wanting to talk with you. Do you have a minute?" Mr. Herrence put his right hand out, directing her toward the Student Services office.

"I'm kind of busy," Maddy said.

"Only a minute. I promise." Mr. Herrence smiled, revealing whitened teeth.

Maddy hefted her backpack. "Okay." In the waiting room, the secretary wore short grey hair and a red blouse. She smiled at Maddy as Maddy followed Mr. Herrence into his office.

"Please, sit down." He closed the door, and sat behind his desk.

Maddy looked out the window, and then at the travel photos on the wall. Mr. Herrence was in each one. She put her bag down and sat.

"There's been a concern expressed, so I thought I'd talk with you face-to-face." He smiled.

Maddy felt a growing sense of dread. *Not more pictures. I don't think I could handle that again.*

"You take your little sister to daycare every morning and pick her up every day after kindergarten."

Where is he going with this? "So?"

"You're often seen with her in Kensington on the weekends." Herrence tapped his lower lip with his forefinger.

Maddy nodded.

"A concern has been expressed that your little sister may

be, in fact, your daughter." He leaned back in his chair, obviously pleased with himself, waiting for her reaction.

Maddy concentrated on breathing. "Who thinks Andrea is my child?"

"I can't disclose that."

Maddy's rage was as instantaneous as it was shocking. "You arrogant asshole! You did this same thing to me when you asked me about the pictures on the net. You wouldn't tell me who found them."

Herrence's face turned red.

"It was you, wasn't it?" Maddy stood, certain of what she had just uncovered.

Herrence's face got redder. "Keep your voice down."

"You told me that it was just between us! That no one else would know. But all the teachers, they knew somehow. All of those comments behind their hands. Those eyes watching me. It was you who told them, wasn't it?" She saw his eyes open wide at the direct hit she'd scored with one sudden insight. "You asshole!"

Herrence said, "Calm down!"

Maddy reached for the door.

"Wait!" Mr. Herrence reached to grab her arm.

Maddy yanked open the door. "Don't you touch me, you bastard! How can you do things like this and live with yourself? You pretend to be all concerned, and then you spread gossip all over the school!" She stepped outside and slammed the door. There was momentary silence. She looked around her. The secretary gave Maddy the thumbs-up.

Maddy looked to her left. Two students sat waiting, their eyes and mouths wide open. Maddy turned back to the secretary. "I forgot my bag."

The secretary smiled. "I'll get it for you."

Maddy waited in the hall just outside of the office, heart pounding, skin tingling. People walked past chatting, totally unaware of the explosive epiphany that had just occurred on the other side of the wall.

The door opened. The secretary stepped out. She held out Maddy's black bag. "Here you go. And thanks."

"Thanks?" Maddy took the bag.

"I've wanted to say that to him for years. Never had the nerve. Glad you did!" The secretary smiled before going back inside.

Maddy looked around to see if there had been any witnesses to the conversation. None came forward. She walked down the hall to the library.

×

"Is there any other option?" Harper's jacket hung off the back of his chair as he sat across from Lane. They were in a one-window office with two chairs and a table.

"We have to start by checking out James Sanders' alibi. If he is, as I suspect, innocent, then we have to verify where he was the night Jennifer disappeared." Lane sketched ideas on a broad sheet of white paper.

Harper tapped the keys on his laptop. He looked over the top of the screen. "Then why did he run?"

"Perhaps because he's the most obvious suspect. And, if he's innocent, then we jumped to the wrong conclusion because he ran. So, we've got to either confirm or eliminate him as a suspect. That means checking out the sports bar." Lane put Jennifer's name at the centre of his diagram and sketched out an approximation of the message on the dumpster that lead them to her body.

"What about Kuldeep? She's telling less than she knows."

Lane drew a circle to one side and put Kuldeep's name in it. "We need to take a close look at the dentists. I'll have to get in touch with McTavish if we don't hear from him today."

Harper looked at the wall behind Lane's head. "We have

to track down the person tagging the dumpsters. I'm beginning to think you were right about that one."

"What do you mean?" Lane looked up from his sketch of a dumpster.

"There are too many questions. That means we have to spend some nights hanging around Kensington, drinking coffee, and watching for someone who paints messages on dumpsters." Harper scratched the side of his face. "Erinn'll be thrilled about that. She still hasn't gotten over us getting shot at."

Lane sat up a little straighter as he was hit by a flashback of blood seeping through a towel.

"I would have paid to see what happened after I dropped you off at the Animal Shelter to meet Roz for the first time. I mean those painkillers really had you goin'." Harper smiled, waiting for a reply.

Lane yawned. "We can't forget about Jennifer's parents. They deserve some answers. That means we really do have to start from the beginning."

×

"You think I'm supposed to talk to you about my customers?" Kuldeep put her hands on her hips. A washcloth hung from her right hand. She looked around the coffee shop, at its lonely tables and chairs and the rearranged stack of newspapers waiting for the next patrons. The mid-morning sky was clear and blue, intensifying Kuldeep's features and accentuating her anxiety.

Lane watched Kuldeep's eyes. They were black with anger. "Where else can we go for information?" he asked. "You're right next door. You listen to the patients who drop in here. You knew Jennifer."

Kuldeep shot him a glare of uncut rage.

Lane felt like stepping back. Instead, he moved forward

half a step. From behind him, he sensed Harper's silent reinforcement.

Kuldeep flicked her washcloth out to the side. It snapped the quiet from the coffee shop. A shaft of sunlight illuminated a cloud of moisture. "You think I don't care about Jennifer? You think I don't worry about my daughter? What am I going to do if I talk and go out of business? Who's going to put my kids through school?"

Harper's laughter began as a chuckle. Lane stepped to one side and turned.

Harper held his left hand over his mouth. His eyes were large. Tears gathered at the corners.

"What's so funny?" Kuldeep's voice hissed with indignation.

"Look at us!" Harper pointed at himself and Lane. "Two big cops are no match for Kuldeep!"

Lane looked at each of them.

Kuldeep smiled. "You enjoyed my performance?"

Later, when the shop was empty again, Kuldeep joined them near the back of the shop at a table next to the washrooms. Harper sipped his coffee, pretending to read the newspaper while entering information on his computer.

Lane sat across from Harper and watched the customers as they came in, waiting to see if he recognized anyone from the dentists' office.

Each time Kuldeep sat down to talk, she revealed a bit more. "It began with my children."

"How's that?" Lane asked.

Harper kept one eye on his computer and another on the front door.

"You'll laugh at me." Kuldeep wrapped her fingers around her teacup.

Lane shrugged. "Try us."

"It's the way Jones looks at my children."

Lane waited.

"When I first moved in here, he would come in to buy juice or tea. He wouldn't talk with me. Grunt maybe, but never talk. Then one day I brought my son with me. He's eight. Jones was really friendly with him, and asked him to come in for a checkup. Then my daughter came in." Kuldeep looked over her shoulder. To make sure the shop was empty.

"What happened?" Lane asked.

"Jones wanted her to come over right away. He told me he would give her a free exam. I said Manpreet was afraid of dentists, he said that was no problem. He would sedate her. All the time he was watching my daughter." Kuldeep looked at the wall as she recalled the experience.

Lane thought, *It's time to bring her back.* "Watching?"

Kuldeep looked directly at him. "The way a man looks at a woman when he wants something."

Harper looked up, his forehead creased.

"Can you be more specific?" Lane asked.

Kuldeep stood up. "Are you stupid?"

"We need to know exactly what you mean, that's all," Lane said.

"Manpreet was like food for a dog."

"I'm not sure I understand," Harper said.

"I don't always have the right words in English." Kuldeep thought for a minute. "Prey? My five-year-old daughter was prey. The dentist kept moving closer. He touched Manpreet's hair in a bad way. Only Manpreet's hair, not my son's. I never bring my youngest daughter here anymore. And my oldest daughter, I never leave her alone in the shop. Sometimes patients come in before an appointment. When they come back afterward, the children are different. Quieter. That was what it was like at first. Now, fewer and fewer people bring their children to the dentist. Still, Dr. Jones and Dr. Stephen, they buy new Mercedes. I work fourteen hours a day. I don't buy a new car. Their office is always empty, and they buy new cars every six months."

"But they're dentists," Harper said.

"Do you have any idea how much I make on each cup of coffee?" Kuldeep looked at Harper and shook her head. "You don't know much about running a business."

×

They stepped through the revolving door. TV screens the size of pool tables featured a variety of sporting events displayed two metres above the floor. Straight ahead, a car skidded, tires smoked, and cars piled into one another. Lane watched the screen as vehicles shed body panels and wheels at over 300 kilometres per hour.

Lane inhaled. *You can just smell the hormones in this place.*

"Used to hang out in places like this when I was nineteen and twenty." Harper looked past the bar at people playing mini-golf.

Lane looked back at the screen. Tire marks etched the track, smoke poured from engines, and rescue workers peeled back twisted body panels to get at drivers. Lane looked down at the photographs of James Sanders. "We'd better get to work." He headed for the bar, noted the bartender's ample cleavage, bleached-blond hair, and tanning-bed skin, then focused on her brown eyes. "We're looking for the manager, please."

The bartender lifted the phone, pressed four numbers and said, "Couple of cops here to see you, Andy."

In less than three minutes, Andy was pumping their hands, offering a table, handing them gift certificates for dinner, and checking out the photos of James Sanders.

Harper pointed at a photo. "We're trying to find out if any-one saw him last Monday. More than a week ago."

Andy tapped his forehead with a forefinger, careful not to

touch his artfully unkempt hair. "Same crew that was on that night is on tonight. Come on, I'll introduce you."

"We bad for business?" Harper asked as they followed in Andy's wake.

Andy stopped, turned, and smiled, then turned around again and began a series of introductions.

They met Julianne twenty minutes later. She wore a red T-shirt that set off her blue eyes. Harper and Lane sat down at a nearby table so they could talk with her at eye level.

Andy's phone rang. He answered it. "I'll be right there." He looked at Lane. "Be right back."

Julianne sat, pushed her blonde shoulder-length hair behind her ears, and studied the photographs. She looked over her shoulder to see if Andy was anywhere nearby. "I work here Monday and Thursday evenings."

"Only two shifts?" Harper asked.

"Money's good. Time goes fast, and my daughter wants to go to Disneyland." Julianne looked them both in the eye.

She's no pushover, be careful, Lane thought.

"Do you remember him at all?" Harper pointed at the picture of James on the table.

She looked at the photo. "He got here around the beginning of my shift. I start at four." Julianne pointed at a table near the front that provided a clear view of the revolving door. "Had his motorcycle helmet on the chair across from him. Kept looking around. Ordered Pepsi. Waited for someone. She never showed."

"She?" Harper pulled out his pocket computer.

Lane watched Julianne's face.

She sensed his attention and turned to study him. "You're not saying much."

"I'm listening." Lane smiled.

Julianne smiled back. "He was waiting for his girlfriend. They've been in here before. She never showed. He was here, waiting, 'til nine or ten that night."

"Is there any way you could confirm the exact time?" Harper tapped the keys on his computer.

"If he paid with a card, there'd be a record of it. I can't remember if he did or not." Julianne looked around. Andy was headed their way. Julianne put her finger on the photo. "He loved her." She stood up.

"How could you tell?" Lane stood.

Julianne shrugged. "He was different around her. Softer. No rough edges. And he never looked at any other women when she was with him."

"Can we get your address and phone number?" Lane asked.

She considered the question, then wrote both on the back of Lane's business card when he slid it across the table.

Andy put his hand on Lane's shoulder. "How's it goin', guys?"

Harper smiled. "We'd better be going."

Lane's phone rang. He waved Andy away. "Hello?"

"Detective Lane?"

Lane recognized the monotone and was instantly angry. "Yes?"

"Dr. Colin Weaver here. We need to meet."

✕

"He said right away." Lane exited the elevator and waited for Harper.

Lane knocked on Dr. Weaver's office door. The opaque glass rattled in its frame.

"Yes?"

Lane looked at Harper. Weaver, or Dr. Fibre as they called him, had always used the same bland tone of voice. But this time there was something uneasy in Fibre's tone.

"It's Lane and Harper." Harper opened the door.

Fibre sat behind the desk, its top shining and reflecting his Hollywood features. He looked at them, before looking away. "Shut the door," he said, and as an afterthought, "please."

Lane still wasn't sure he would be able to control his anger after what Fibre had said to Christine.

Sensing this, Harper said, "You asked to see us."

Fibre looked at Lane, looked at the floor, then looked at his computer screen. "I have results from the autopsy and tests completed on the remains of Jennifer Towers."

Lane waited.

Harper said, "And?"

"There is one major anomaly. At first I believed Ms. Towers died of asphyxiation, but the bruising was minor and there were no other signs of a struggle. This is very unusual. Victims almost always fight to breathe. In this case, it appears she did not." Fibre played with the computer. Lines appeared across his forehead.

"What do you think now?" Harper asked.

"I'm not sure." Fibre shook his head and frowned. "Because she worked in a dental office there is one likely possibility."

Harper waited a minute before asking, "Well?'

"Nitrous oxide. It is difficult to trace. Because there is no obvious evidence of the cause of death in this case, it is the most likely solution." Fibre shifted his weight in his chair and avoided eye contact.

"Could we get a copy of the report?" Harper asked.

Fibre looked at Harper as if he'd just appeared in the room. "Of course." He turned back to the computer, and the printer began to whir. Paper stuck its tongue out of the printer.

Lane watched Fibre. There was sweat running down the side of his face. *Fibre never sweats. Especially not in here; it must be fifteen degrees*, Lane thought.

Harper picked up the paper from the printer. He turned to leave.

Lane began to stand.

"There's something else." Fibre said, and waited until they sat back down.

What else could there be? Lane thought.

Fibre lifted his eyes, made contact with Lane's, then looked back at the floor. "What I said to your niece was unconscionable. I had no reason for saying that to her. I pride myself in being fair-minded. But what I said was…"

"Way out of line?" Harper asked.

Fibre looked up. Rage flared in his eyes, but was instantly extinguished. "It's not easy for me. This is very difficult. I'm good with analysis. Living, breathing people are incomprehensible to me. Women are unfathomable."

"My niece came from a religious compound where the men treated her like she was less than human. Her mother let them do that to her daughter. We're trying to build my niece's confidence back up again. Trying to help her feel good about herself." Lane stopped. *I would never have imagined having this kind of conversation with Fibre.*

The doctor sat back, shrinking in the chair. "There are no words."

Harper stood up. Lane did the same.

Fibre watched them with eyes that appeared more child-like than adult.

"Thanks for the information," Harper said.

"One other thing. We may have DNA evidence. A hair sample was found between layers of the plastic wrap. The hair did not belong to Ms. Towers. The plastic was the kind of product used to wrap and preserve food." Weaver looked at the floor.

Lane closed the door behind them. Neither spoke until they got into the car. Lane said, "That was an unusual experience."

"I've never seen him like that. He was so," Harper searched for the right word, "human."

Lane lifted his head, staring at nothing in particular, struck by the truth of Harper's observation and the mixed feelings he had about Fibre.

×

"How did it start?" Lane asked.

"I don't know. She called him Quasimodo, and he called her a Barbie."

Both listened to the unusual quiet in the house. Christine and Matt had barricaded themselves in their rooms. Roz lay on the floor between Arthur and Lane. She snored. The men looked at her.

Arthur rubbed Roz's ears. "How are we going to handle this thing on Saturday?"

"Thing?"

Arthur glared at Lane. "You know, Christine meeting her dad."

"Maybe it'll handle itself?" *Did I really say that?* Lane thought.

Arthur looked at Lane like he'd just farted in the mayor's office. "Her father hasn't ever seen her. As far as we know, he's never tried to find her. Her mother has rejected her. Do I have to paint you a picture of how devastating this entire experience could be for her?"

Lane thought before answering. "No, you've already managed to paint a pretty clear picture."

"So, what are we going to do?"

A number of possibilities ran through Lane's mind. "We all have to be there."

"In his present state of mind, Matt will probably refuse."

"And we have to go out for dinner first." Lane smiled when he thought of where they would be eating.

×

Maddy carried Andrea in her arms. Andrea whimpered and sucked her thumb.

"I'm sorry Andrea. I'm tired too. I shouldn't have said that." Maddy felt an overwhelming sense of guilt after her outburst.

Andrea put her head on Maddy's shoulder.

"You're getting to be such a big girl." *And heavy*, Maddy thought. She tried to concentrate on something else to take her mind off of the weight of her sister. The spray cans and oversized pens rattled up against one another in her backpack. She listened to the sounds they made as she walked across the school field. When she stepped onto the teachers' paved parking lot, she checked for lights in her house at the end of the cul-de-sac. The light from the TV illuminated the window in the living room.

"Shit." A cloud of frosty breath followed the words. She put her cheek against Andrea's to warm them both.

Maddy made her way around the back of the house, wondering if it would be possible to get upstairs without alerting whoever was still up.

She managed to open the back door, pull the key from her pocket, and balance Andrea. Down the hall, the polished floor reflected the drama playing out on the TV in the living room. Maddy kicked off her shoes and slipped down the hall until she could see her mother on the couch. Her feet stuck out from the blanket she'd pulled down from the back of the couch. Maddy moved closer. Andrea sucked her thumb furiously. Maddy caught the sour smell of alcohol seeping from her mother's pores.

Maddy took Andrea in her arms and went upstairs to bed.

chapter 11

"Detectives Lane and Harper to see James Sanders." Harper spoke into the intercom on the third floor of the Foothills Medical Centre. They stood outside the locked grey metal door and waited.

A buzzer sounded, and Lane pulled the door open. They walked past the nursing station. Four pairs of eyes followed them as they walked down to the end of the hall and into the last room on the right.

She's the last person I expected to find here, Lane thought. "Mrs. Towers?" He took in the room. James was in the bed next to the window. His broken leg was propped up on a pillow. James was caught in the motion of changing the channel on the overhead television. At the foot of the bed, MaryAnne looked up from the mystery novel she was reading. To Lane it looked as if she'd dropped twenty pounds on a diet of grief.

MaryAnne said, "He's resting."

"It's okay." James propped himself on an elbow so he could see the detectives a bit better. He used a ruler to scratch his multicoloured leg.

Harper moved to Lane's left. "One of the waitresses at the sports bar told us that she saw you there the night Jennifer disappeared. We're here to go over what you remember about that day."

MaryAnne put her book down.

She almost smiled, Lane thought.

James looked from one detective to the other.

"I think they're saying they believe you, James." MaryAnne got up and stood next to the window.

"Please, take us through that day." Lane stood at the foot of the bed so he could gauge James' reactions.

Harper moved so that he could observe MaryAnne.

"I called her at lunchtime to say we should meet at the bar so I could apologize and buy her dinner." James looked at MaryAnne.

"Apologize?" Lane studied James' eyes.

"I called her father an asshole." James glanced at Mary-Anne.

Harper and Lane waited.

"Jenn was going to meet me around three-thirty or four o'clock. She wasn't sure how long her last appointment would take." James put his head back on the pillow and stared at the ceiling.

"What time did you arrive?" Harper asked.

"Got let off of work early. Got there about three-fifteen. I waited 'til ten o'clock and drove by the office. Her car was still there, but the place was closed. I went home."

"Did you have any contact with her after that?" Lane looked at MaryAnne.

She looked directly back at Lane without blinking.

"I tried her cell and home phone but there was no answer." James shrugged.

MaryAnne said, "We were out for dinner. She always lets us know when she's going somewhere. Usually, she phones after work and leaves a message. When she wasn't home the next morning, we dropped by her work. The car was covered with frost."

"What about her attitude toward her job?" Lane asked, thinking, *Maybe this will get us closer to what happened.*

"She was looking for another one. Jennifer had some feelers out with friends she'd graduated with." MaryAnne looked out the window and wiped at her eyes.

Lane watched her reflection in the window. She lifted

her head and looked back at him through the shadow of her reflected body.

MaryAnne sniffed. "Things started off quite well at Jones' practice. Then she started to complain about little things. She wondered why there were so few patients. The receptionist, Ramona, didn't talk much and made Jenn feel like she wasn't welcome. And she couldn't figure out why Dr. Stephen was away so often. At least four days out of five, he'd be gone. It just didn't feel right, and she started to think she'd better look for another job."

"Any specifics?" Harper sat down on the empty bed next to James and pulled out his pocket computer.

"It's like smoke," James said.

Lane focused all of his attention on James. "Explain."

"Jennifer knew there was something wrong there, she could smell it, she could feel it." James stopped talking to look at MaryAnne.

"We've been talking about it ever since. We just haven't come up with any definite answers." MaryAnne looked at James. "He gets tired quickly."

Lane and Harper were back in their car within fifteen minutes.

Harper started the engine. "Smoke?"

Lane watched a husband and wife carefully put a newborn in a car seat. "It's possible Jennifer discovered the source of the smoke."

×

Fibre sounded like he was talking on speakerphone. "We're still no closer to an answer. Toxicology came back inconclusive. I'm still eliminating possibilities one by one."

To Lane's ear, Fibre could have been talking about the weather or whether to have the filet mignon or the salmon for dinner. *It's a good thing the good doctor is great at his job,*

Lane thought.

"I'm looking at contaminants in the victim's system, but so far nothing has come up. Not even a little alcohol, although there was some evidence of caffeine." Fibre came as close as he ever did to sounding frustrated. "Is there another specific avenue that I might want to explore?"

Lane searched his thoughts for possibilities. "What other possibilities besides nitrous oxide are there?"

"I can't think of any," Fibre said.

"The dental office is called Rockwell Sedation Dentistry," Lane said.

"We keep coming back to nitrous oxide," Fibre said.

"What do you know about it?" Lane asked.

"Nitrous oxide is commonly called laughing gas. I'll check into the typical anesthetics used by dentists in general and those used at the offices of…?"

"Doctors Stephen and Jones," Lane said.

Fibre hung up.

chapter 12

Lane watched the BMW driver ahead of them change lanes, turn left without signaling, then run the three-way stop inside the mall parking lot.

"Did you see that?" Christine asked from the back seat.

Matt sat next to Lane in the front passenger seat. He exhaled and looked out his window.

"See what?" Arthur asked from the back.

"That?" Matt pointed at the blue sedan. The luxury vehicle stopped and parked. The driver hopped out and ran into a sporting goods store. His BMW blocked traffic.

Lane turned right, away from the congestion.

He parked at the very southern edge of the shopping mall parking lot. *Away from the madness,* he thought.

After they got out of the Jeep and walked past the rows of parked cars, a horn sounded.

"Look!" Matt pointed.

The man was getting back into the BMW parked out front of the sporting goods. A horn sounded again. The man turned around and raised his middle finger to the person in the car behind the BMW.

"Let them sort it out," Arthur said to Lane.

Lane waited for Christine and Arthur to catch up. Matt ambled along in his patented cerebral palsy gallop that was somewhere between walking and skipping.

"Thanks." Arthur touched Lane's elbow.

They gathered inside where some shoppers reclined in oversized, overstuffed chairs and others ambled east and west. Lane caught the scent of coffee and looked to his right.

A gaggle of men and women gathered near the espresso machine that alternatively steamed and hissed out lattes, mochas, and cappuccinos. "Which way are you going? I'll catch up to you. Anybody else want a coffee?" Lane asked.

"I'll help you carry them," Matt said and went with Lane to join the line.

Arthur and Christine turned right, toward a series of shops where, as Matt put it, "Everyone comes away lighter in the pocketbook."

After ordering their drinks, Lane sat in a box-shaped armchair. Matt sat on the armrest.

"Think she'll be okay?" Matt asked.

But you two fight so much. I thought you hated each other, Lane thought. He stared at Matt. The eyes of his nephew looked back at him, waiting for an answer.

Lane glanced at a young woman with black hair who was making coffee.

"Go ahead, just say it." Matt put his hand on his uncle's shoulder.

"I thought you two hated one another." Lane looked up to gauge Matt's reaction.

Matt laughed. "You worry too much. She's like the sister I never had. Almost everyone I talk with at school fights with their sisters. It's the way it is."

"Mochas and cappuccinos double up!" The voice sounded like that of an auctioneer.

"That's us!" Lane stood up. The chair tilted. Matt almost fell off the armrest.

Holding two coffees each, they looked for signs of Arthur and Christine.

Two white-haired mall walkers passed by with arms swinging and legs pumping in military precision.

"You don't like talking about it, do you?" Matt asked while sipping his coffee and looking at Lane over the rim.

"About what?"

With whipped cream on his top lip, Matt smiled. "About family stuff. You used to talk before, now you just clam up."

"Before?" Lane asked.

"Before Christine came. Before that we used to talk all of the time. Now we hardly talk at all." Matt looked away.

And he's listening to every word I say, Lane thought. "Before, I thought I knew what to say to you. Now it's different. There's so much tension all the time. And…"

Matt waited for half a minute. "Well?"

"When my sister had Christine, I was there when she was born. We bonded. Then she was gone. I was gone. Now she's back. I still don't know quite how to handle that. There are years of her life that I know nothing about. And I'm worried about you. Worried about saying the wrong thing. Worried you're unhappy because she's living with us. She seems so confused. I have no idea what to say to either of you." Lane looked at Matt, who was looking through a window, past the mannequins.

They watched as Arthur picked out a blouse for Christine. The look she gave him was sharp enough to cut flesh. Arthur raised his eyebrows and hung the clothing back on the rack.

"You think other families don't act like that?" Matt pointed with his finger and the cup of coffee. "Sometimes I sit in the mall just watching how families act."

"I have no idea what other families do." Lane wondered how long it would be before Christine left the store, and some drama would play itself out in the middle of the mall.

"I've been asking around."

Lane turned to Matt. "And?"

"Everybody thinks their families are pretty screwed up. Some parents get drunk every weekend. Some pay absolutely no attention to their kids. And some keep their kids so close they can hardly breathe."

They watched as Christine began to walk out of the store, followed by Arthur.

"Here we go." Lane prepared for the explosion.

"You worry too much," Matt said.

Christine turned toward them.

"I thought it would look good on you," Arthur said.

"I hate that colour!" Christine rolled her eyes and shook her head.

Arthur took a deep breath and looked at Lane as if to say, "You try."

"What colours do you like?" Lane asked.

"I don't know," Christine shrugged.

Matt said, "You like that place over there." Matt pointed with one cup of coffee while handing Arthur the other.

Lane handed Christine a cup. "Let's give it a try," he said. "What do you think?"

Christine looked around her.

Matt said, "You might like that one." Matt pointed at a window hiding the opening to another clothing shop.

"It's too expensive." Christine looked further down the mall.

"How many times do you get to meet your dad for the first time?" Arthur asked.

"Let's give it a try." Matt headed for the store without looking to see if anyone was following. He moved with none of Christine's grace.

Lane tucked his arm in Christine's and Arthur took her by the other elbow.

As they turned past the display window, they came face-to-face with a copper-coloured waterfall reaching from the floor to the ceiling.

It's much the same as the one in Dr. Jones' office, Lane thought.

Inside, the mid-sized shop was filled with a major collection of female shoppers, all of whom turned to look at Christine being escorted by an all-male entourage. Lane felt Christine try to turn around, but he and Arthur carried her forward into the centre of the store and the heart of the crowd.

"How about that?" Lane looked at a simple white blouse and black pants. He caught a whiff of perfume and strawberry shampoo emanating from one of the women.

Christine moved in closer to touch the fabric.

A woman walked past Lane. She smiled. "You're a brave man."

Christine held the top and pants up to her as she stood in front of the mirror. "It's 50 percent off."

Five minutes later, they passed the waterfall again. Lane heard the trickle of the water and an idea lapped at the back of his mind. He looked back at the crowd inside the store and wondered at the cost of the sculptured waterfall, rent, salaries, and sales. *It must take a fortune to operate this place. Kuldeep was right; I don't understand what it costs to run a business.*

"Now you need some shoes to go with the outfit." Arthur swung the bag holding Christine's clothes, pointing in the direction of a nearby shoe store.

All were relieved when the point came when Christine said, "These shoes are a perfect match for the outfit."

They were home within the hour.

×

At the entrance to the Red and White Club, Lane watched Christine as she opened the door for the TV crew. He thought, *White and black never looked so elegant.* He reflected on a memory of her when she was less than an hour old.

The TV personality was blonde and wore a tight red top and matching skirt. Her high heels seemed to clap, "Watch me!" as she stepped onto the tiled lobby. The echo of stiletto applause followed her. The camera operator said, "Thank you," to Christine.

Arthur, Matt, and Lane followed, taking in the room. The carpeted ballroom was filled with tables, red tablecloths, and life-sized images of Bobbie "Go Long" Green posing with a football, posing at the goal line, making a fingertip catch with outstretched arms, and waving to the crowd.

Lane looked around the room. He felt Christine tuck her arm around his.

Matt watched them, waiting.

Arthur cocked his head to the left.

Lane followed the motion.

The lights of three TV cameras illuminated one man. He stood more than six feet tall. His smile was directed mainly at the reporter in the red dress. Lane studied the man he'd met only a couple of times nearly twenty years ago. Bobbie's black hair was still thick and cut short. He moved like he was comfortable and confident in his skin. The blue pinstriped suit was obviously tailored to fit his body.

"That's him?" Christine asked.

Lane nodded. "That's your father."

They moved closer to catch the questions and answers.

"What are you up to these days, Mr. Green?" the reporter in the red dress asked. She looked up at Bobbie, fluttered her eyelashes, and smiled.

Bobbie grinned, "I've got various business interests around the country. They keep me busy, and of course I play a little golf when I can."

"How does it feel to be back here?" another reporter asked.

"Great. It's a great honour to have my name next to so many other talented players, and to see some people I haven't seen in years." Bobbie looked over the crowd, spotted Lane, stared for a moment, frowned, then looked away.

"So, you're her." The female voice came from the right of Lane and Christine.

They turned to the woman behind the voice. She stood as tall as Christine, and had the same colour eyes and hair. Even her skin was a similar shade.

Besides that, Lane thought, *their faces are remarkably similar.* He felt himself fill with dread at what the woman was about to say.

"How old are you?" the woman asked.

"Eighteen." Christine studied the woman's face and clothes.

"My name is Arthur." Arthur held out his hand.

She took it, smiled and said, "Alexandra Green."

"This is Christine." Arthur put his hand on Christine's shoulder.

Christine held out her hand. Alexandra pushed it aside and hugged her. She put the flat of her hand on Christine's spine and rubbed it furiously. "Bit of a shock for both of us. My mother mentioned you a time or two. Dad always said it wasn't true, but one of the wives on the team was certain. When my parents got into an argument, you usually came up."

Lane's mouth went dry. "How old are you?"

"Nineteen," Alexandra said.

Christine stepped back and wiped at her eyes. "This is my Uncle Lane and my cousin, Matt."

"Good to meet you." Alexandra's long fingers wrapped around Lane's hand.

"You look so much alike." Lane heard the quiver in his voice. Alexandra held onto his hand as if trying to steady him.

"I've been watching you since you came in. You see, I don't have any brothers or sisters, so I've always wondered about you. It's one of the reasons I came on this trip: to see if you would be here." Alexandra kept her eyes on Christine.

Christine shivered and looked over at the TV lights.

"Want to meet our father?" Alexandra grabbed Christine's hand and pulled her forward.

"Wait!" Lane felt an overwhelming sense of foreboding. He moved to catch Christine, but the young women were beyond his reach and fast approaching the edge of the cameras. Christine used her free hand to shield her eyes from the glare as the girls entered the spotlight.

"Stop them!" Arthur pulled at Lane's elbow.

Lane felt he was watching a catastrophe about to occur, and there was nothing he could do but observe.

"Too late!" Matt said, standing at Lane's other elbow.

The cameras turned to the young women. The reporter in the red dress turned to Bobbie, "Are you going to introduce your daughters?"

The look Bobbie gave his oldest daughter caused both young women to stop and look away. "No comment," Bobbie Green said. He walked away from his daughters, away from the cameras, and out of the room.

Christine said nothing all the way home. Once inside the house, she went to her room and closed the door.

Arthur passed the time rocking in the chair next to the couch. He looked at the grandfather clock. "She's been in there for over four hours."

"It was another rejection." Lane looked at Roz, whose worried eyes told the story of their evening.

"I gave her our number and address." Arthur looked out the window as a car drove by.

"What?" Lane asked.

"I gave Alexandra our phone number and our address before we left." Arthur waited for Lane's reaction. "Maybe when things get back to normal...you know."

Lane thought, *I'm beginning to wonder if our lives will ever get back to normal.*

"Well, one thing is for sure, this night can't get any worse," Arthur said.

The phone rang eight minutes later. Lane picked it up, "Hello?"

"Uncle Lane? It's Mandy. You know, your niece. My parents don't know I'm calling. Your father is in the Foothills Medical Centre. The priest is giving him the last rites. You should come." Mandy took a breath.

"I don't know if I should." Lane felt an old agony intensifying somewhere just beneath his ribs.

"He asked me to phone you."

"Who did?" Lane asked.

"Your father."

I haven't seen him in more than fifteen years, Lane thought. "What room is he in?" he asked.

She told him and hung up.

Arthur said, "What is it?"

"Dad is dying, and he's asking for me." Lane studied the patterns in the oak of their living-room floor. He saw how the wood grain of some boards seemed to run into the next even though most of them were of different shades, ranging from blonde to something close to cherry.

Arthur grabbed Lane by the shoulders. "I'll stay here with the kids. You have to go."

Lane looked up.

"Go." Arthur kissed him.

×

Lane parked on the east side of the hospital, looked at the moon in the clear sky, eased past a man in a wheelchair who was smoking a cigarette, walked into the warm air blasting between two sets of sliding automatic glass doors, and was enveloped by the soapy, antiseptic scent of the Foothills Medical Centre.

He shared the elevator with two nurses, who stared at the door all the way up.

In the hallway he checked the signs, walked past the nursing station, and found the room at the end of the north wing. He read the name, Martin Lane, on the wall. *Am I too late?*

"Yes?" asked a woman's voice.

He looked into the eyes of a strawberry blonde who was still quite attractive in her middle years. Lane recognized her at about the same moment she realized who she was talking to.

"It's you," she said, and looked over her shoulder.

Lane stepped to his left and looked inside the room. He saw his brother at the foot of the bed. Joseph Lane wore a blue pinstriped suit. *It's like a lawyer's uniform,* Lane thought.

Joseph turned his eyes to his brother and stared.

Lane was shocked by how much he and his brother looked alike — except, of course, for their hair. Joseph had none.

"We weren't expecting…" Margaret began, as she slipped past Lane to put herself between the brothers.

"You to be here," Joseph finished.

Lane recalled their habit of finishing each other's sentences. *Say as little as possible,* Lane thought, *and protect Mandy.*

"How did you find out?" Margaret smiled with her teeth.

Take the offensive. Realizing he was being tag-teamed and put on the defensive, Lane smiled back and asked, "How's he doing?" Lane nodded toward the shrunken form under the sheet.

Margaret's eyes flashed with anger. He watched her hide it behind a smile. "We know why you're here." It was an accusation.

Lane thought, *You have no idea, sister.* He eased around her.

Joseph held out his hand. Lane shook it out of habit. The flesh felt oddly unfamiliar. Joseph released his brother, and stepped back closer to the wall.

Lane looked at the man in the bed. His eyes were closed. His nose was larger somehow, his eyebrows thicker, more unruly, than Lane remembered. White hair stuck out at odd angles over his ears and against the pillow. The skin on his neck lay in loose folds, like chicken flesh. Lane estimated his father weighed no more than one hundred and twenty pounds and was now under six feet tall. The lack of medical machinery, told Lane that no resuscitation was requested.

Martin's blue eyes opened. They registered fear.

"He's here," Joseph said.

Lane could feel Margaret's disapproval like cold breath at the back of his neck.

It took more than a few short sniffs of oxygen before Martin recognized Lane.

Lane reminded himself to breathe.

"It *is* you." Martin's voice came in quick gasps.

Lane had a flashback of his father smoking a cigarette. He looked at his father's fingers and saw the yellow stain of nicotine on the thumb and forefinger of his right hand.

"How did skating go today?" Martin asked.

"I…" Lane looked at his brother and sister-in-law. They would not meet his eyes. "Fine."

"Good. You're such a fine skater. Sorry I didn't get to your practice again today." Martin watched Lane's face carefully.

"That's okay. Maybe next time." Lane thought, *He's remembering the figure skating lessons. That was so long ago. He's lost his short-term memory.*

"Sit with me awhile?" Martin lifted his right hand with the intravenous tube and patted the side of the bed. "Tell me how you're doing."

Lane sat down. He remembered his father's scent. The mixture of scotch and tobacco. Tonight, he smelled of urine.

Martin waved his left hand, "You two can go home now, he's here."

Margaret said, "We'll stay with you." She looked at her husband.

"We'll stay," Joseph said.

"We'll be fine! Go!" Martin began to cough.

Margaret opened her mouth.

Lane watched Joseph wink and shake his head. "We'll go downstairs for a bite to eat." He took Margaret's arm to guide her out the door. She pulled her arm away.

Lane watched them leave. He saw Margaret hovering, her image reflected in the glass of the storage-room door across the hall. She perched outside the door, listening.

Lane watched his father sipping short breaths once his coughing subsided.

A woman walked in. She filled the doorway. "Time for physio."

Lane watched as she rolled his father onto his side, massaged his back, then worked his arms and legs. "There you go. Now you can go on with your visit." Lane watched her leave.

When he looked back toward the bed, his father's eyes were on him.

"Seems like you're so busy, I never see you anymore. You're always skating or up in your room doing homework," Martin said.

Lane remembered those days when he became aware that there might be something quite different about him. Something that needed to be hidden. That uncertainty, gradually turning into certainty. And, with that knowledge, Lane withdrew, hiding from those who knew him the best. Those he felt he could no longer trust. Lane nodded at the memory.

"I remember how you could skate. I thought you were flying. The way you moved! It was something!" Martin, unaware he had lost the concept of time, looked past Lane at the wall, where the scene replayed somewhere in the depths of memory, in a world where the more recent past no longer existed.

Somewhere in that memory, Lane's father fell asleep.

Lane looked out of the window at the lights of the city spread out to the horizon. He looked east along the river valley to the Louise Bridge and Kensington. He decided to sit for a few minutes and close his eyes.

He woke up when the physiotherapist returned. She said, "Didn't mean to wake you."

She leaned over the bed and began to work on Martin's back.

Lane sat up in his chair. He licked his lips then searched his pocket for a pack of gum.

The physiotherapist lifted Martin's arm. "Wait a minute!" She dropped the arm.

"What's the matter?" Lane asked.

"My goodness!" She looked at Lane. He saw the fear in her eyes.

Lane stood up and looked at his father, who appeared to have sunken into the pillows.

"Cold. He's cold," she said.

Lane reached out to touch his father's foot where it poked out from underneath the blanket. "He's dead?"

She nodded.

Margaret stepped into the room. "We'll take it from here," she said.

Joseph followed in her wake. He studied Lane with vague eyes.

chapter 13

The phone rang just as Matt, Lane, and Arthur sat down to lunch.

They stopped and looked at one another across the table before Lane reached for the phone.

"Hello?"

"It's Alexandra."

He felt his mind slowly working at processing information, exploring options.

"Can I talk with Christine?" Alexandra asked.

"We can't get her to come out of her room." Lane looked across the table at Arthur.

Matt said, "It's no wonder. First her mother, and then her father."

"Could I come over?" Alexandra asked.

"And your father?" Lane didn't think before asking the question. He thought, *It's like my mind and mouth are disconnected.*

"I just put him on the airplane. He's gone home."

Lane rubbed his palm over his face to try to clear his muddled mind. "When will you be here?"

"An hour."

Lane hung up. He looked at Arthur, then Matt. "She says she'll be here in an hour."

"Who?" Matt and Arthur asked.

"Alexandra," Lane said.

All three looked up in the direction of Christine's room.

"You tell her," Arthur said to Lane.

"I'll tell her." Matt stood up.

Lane and Arthur watched him move to the stairs.

"Are you going to be okay?" Arthur asked Lane.

Lane tried to think of an answer.

Roz whined at the back door to be let out.

"Smart dog. You know when trouble is coming." Lane got up and opened the door. Roz nosed her way outside. *Maybe I should follow you*, he thought.

The sound of Matt tapping on Christine's door carried down the stairs. A few seconds later, he tapped again. "Christine, I'm opening the door."

He might need backup. Lane made his way to the bottom of the stairs. He stubbed his toe on the bottom step. The pain brought him some sense of clarity, or at least clarity about the pain.

Matt opened the door, stepped inside, and closed it behind him.

Lane anticipated an explosion of emotion from his niece.

There was the murmur of Matt's voice and mumbled one-word answers from Christine.

Then, "She is? An hour! Why didn't you tell me?"

Matt stepped outside, looked at Lane, and smiled. "She's says she's getting ready."

Matt, Arthur, and Lane sipped coffee and listened with more than a little curiosity while Christine showered, dried, and stomped back and forth between her bedroom and the bathroom. Even Roz ventured back inside to await the unveiling.

They watched as Christine came downstairs in a T-shirt and jeans. She poured herself a cup of coffee and nibbled on a blueberry muffin. "What are you lookin' at?" She asked as she accidentally spit a muffin crumb, which plopped into Arthur's cup. Lane watched the event with curious detachment. Arthur, unaware, sipped his coffee.

The doorbell rang eight minutes after Christine finished her coffee. Christine answered it.

Alexandra waited for the door to open, stepped inside, and embraced Christine.

"I just dropped Dad off at the airport. I decided to stay on for a few days." Alexandra said into Christine's ear. "Do you want to go shopping?"

Christine said, "Matt? You comin'?"

Matt frowned at Lane and Arthur. "Okay."

"Would you like to come back here for supper?" Arthur asked.

The sisters looked at one another. Alexandra said, "Sure."

After they left, Arthur turned to Lane, "What are you going to do?"

"About what?" Lane's mind filled with the image of his father in his hospital bed, with a mind falling deeper into the past.

"About the funeral."

×

"Maddy, I'm hungry."

"Shit." Maddy reached inside her coat pocket to pull out the fifty she'd taken from her mother's purse.

Andrea started to cry.

Maddy took a breath, leaned over, and hugged her sister. Andrea wrapped her arms around Maddy's neck. She looked at the group of three approaching her: two young women and a young man. He walked with a bit of a limp. *The women are absolutely stunning,* Maddy thought. A river of resentment washed over her as her little sister hugged her closer.

"They're gay then?" The young woman with the accent asked.

Maddy thought, *She's American.*

"Got a problem with that?" the young man asked.

The American leaned her head back and laughed. "Look at me." She pointed at her face. "Look at her." She touched the shoulder of the young woman next to her. Then, she laughed harder. "Look at you!" She pointed at the young man, who began to laugh. "How could the three of us have a problem with anything? Come on Christine, we've got shoes to buy and we need lattes for fuel," the American said.

Maddy watched them pass. *Some people have it all,* she thought. "Come on," she said to Andrea, "we'll go to your favourite: the Mexican restaurant."

She looked ahead at a pair of young men headed in the opposite direction. *Be careful,* she thought and held Andrea's hand a little tighter.

The teens were dressed in black jeans and jackets of a related style. They wore similar hats and had similar walks. Both wore dragon tattoos on the backs of their right hands.

Maddy watched as other pedestrians furtively appraised the teens with heightened senses, evidenced by their stiffer backs and sideways glances.

Maddy looked straight ahead as the pair approached.

The male on the right asked his buddy, "Do you use moisturizer?"

The one on the left said, "No."

"Man, you should. Look at your hands. Now, look at mine." He held his hands out in front of him as he passed Maddy and Andrea.

In the wake of the gangsters, Maddy inhaled the scent of lavender and aftershave.

The sisters waited at the pedestrian crossing. Andrea pressed the button. Yellow lights flashed. They waited for a cyclist, who used his right hand to push his knee on the down stroke of the pedal. He smiled as he rolled through the crosswalk and said, "Thanks."

✕

"We're going out." Arthur wore black pants and a fresh-pressed blue shirt. He pulled on his leather jacket.

"What?" Lane sat close to the phone.

"A month ago, Loraine and Lisa invited us to their baby's christening. Get up. We're going." Arthur bent to put on a shoe.

"I forgot." Lane closed his eyes as he realized his mistake.

Arthur stood up and frowned. "Of course you did." He bent back down to tie his other shoe. "The kids are out. They know your cell number, and we haven't been out together for months. Let's go."

It took less than half an hour to get to Lisa and Loraine's inner city bungalow, where the family had just returned from baby Benjamin's baptism. "He screamed through the whole thing," Lisa said, holding his left hand as she breast-fed him in the front room, surrounded by a talkative mixture of friends and family. "Did you get some lobster?" Lisa asked Kane and Arthur, "Loraine's dad sent it from the east coast. Lots of beer and coleslaw to go along with it." She looked back down at her son and stroked his cheek.

Lane thought, *Lisa, the big tough Mountie. Now her son's got her wrapped around his finger. Come to think of it, Matt and Christine have got us wrapped around theirs!*

Arthur handed a gift to a beaming Loraine, who sat across from her partner and son. Loraine, the blonde-haired psychologist, was just over half the height of her partner. Arthur had informed Lane on the way over that the gift of baby clothing had been purchased and wrapped two weeks ago. Loraine hugged Arthur around the neck, and said, "Go get some lobster before it's gone."

Loraine spotted Lane and stood on her toes to hug him as he bent to hug her back. "So glad you could make it. Isn't Benjamin beautiful?"

Lane nodded. "Lisa's turned into an earth mother."

Loraine smiled. "She can't believe it, and neither can I. He's perfect." She put her hands on either side of Lane's face and kissed him. Then she went to Lisa and kissed her.

Lane met Arthur out on the covered deck. The floor was covered with a blue tarp. People sat in lawn chairs with newspaper on their laps and at their feet as they struggled with lobster claws, stuffed lobster meat into their mouths, or sat with eyes glazed from eating too much lobster. Many wore green garbage bags over their torsos. Lane thought, *It looks like some weird, campy version of Robin Hood.* He looked for Errol Flynn; instead, he spotted an old acquaintance, an architect named Robert, who actually could have passed for Flynn. Robert waved Lane over.

Once Lane found his newspaper, paper plate, lobster, coleslaw, and cold beer from the ice-filled cooler in the middle of the floor, he sat down in the lawn chair next to Robert.

"It's been a long time," Robert said.

Lane cracked the shell of a lobster's tail by locking his fingers and making a vice with his palms. "How's business?" Lane asked as he peeled the outer skeleton, removed the meat, and dipped it in a nearby bowl of vinegar.

"Lots of money around town these days. I'm always in the inner city designing something glitzy for someone wanting to tear down an old house and erect a palace with lots of exotic wood, pillars, granite countertops, and arched entryways. It's becoming a bit of a cliché, I'm afraid." Robert took a sip of white wine.

Lane took a bite of lobster and thought, *I'd forgotten how good this tastes.* He looked at Robert, who managed to look elegant even when he was sitting in a lawn chair and sipping wine from a beer glass. Lane looked across at Arthur, who was talking with Loraine's brother and dipping morsels of lobster in butter.

"How are you enjoying your new house?" Robert asked.

"The house is fine."

"Word has it you've inherited two children." Robert chuckled. "You and Arthur have initiated quite a trend among your friends."

Lane laughed. "This is the first social outing we've had in months, and we've got the cell phone just in case."

"How old are your niece and nephew?" Robert asked.

"Eighteen and seventeen." Lane picked up his bottle of honey brewed beer and took a sip.

"An interesting age."

"You could say that." Lane leaned over, picked up a knife, and split open one of the lobster's claws on the chopping block. He fished out the white flesh with his thumb and index finger.

"I have a few nieces and nephews and when I talk with their parents it makes me glad I'm not of the breeding persuasion."

Lane considered the remark as he savoured the lobster and took another taste of beer. "Since they arrived on our doorstep, it's been…"

"Insane, wonderful, bizarre, hopeless, chaotic, magical?" Robert asked.

"Actually, all of that and much more."

"And you're working on another interesting case, I hear?" Robert handed Lane a paper napkin.

"You certainly are well informed." Lane wiped his fingers and face.

"It's a small town. All I have to do is listen."

"This case concerns a young woman who worked in a dentist's office." Lane leaned back in his chair and thought about grabbing another lobster.

"Now there's a 'Jones' who definitely dares the neighbours to keep up with him," Robert said.

"You know Dr. Jones?" Lane looked over at a grinning Robert.

He lifted his glass. "Dr. and Mrs. Jones wanted an ostentatious home. I designed one for them."

"You enjoyed working with the doctor?" Lane forgot all about the lobster as he listened carefully to Robert's response.

"He has a very orderly mind and exotic tastes." Robert's tone was a combination of scandalous intrigue and sarcasm.

"Exotic tastes in?" Lane dangled the hook to see if Robert would reach for the bait.

"Young — very young — women."

Lane nodded. "He revealed his predilections to you?"

Robert took a sip of wine. "No. At least not in words."

Lane waited, tired of Robert's game.

Robert leaned over, picked up the bottle of wine next to his chair, and poured himself half a glass. "Let's just say he has an eye for prepubescent females. I don't have any proof, you understand. It was the way he looked at his youngest daughter. It was like smoke in the room. You can smell what's going on, but it would be very difficult to prove that the doctor intends to bed his youngest."

A lobster on a paper plate appeared under Lane's nose. He looked to his left.

Loraine stood grinning, with baby Ben on her right arm. "Have another one. They don't fly in that often."

"Sit here." Robert stood up. "I need to chat with Lisa about the plans for your basement."

"How are Christine and Matt doing?" Loraine asked as she sat down. Ben burped. Lane smiled, and so did Loraine.

Loraine lifted the baby to her shoulder and patted Ben on the back. He opened his blue eyes for a minute then spit up some of his lunch. It dribbled down the tea towel Loraine had draped over her shoulder.

"He threw up." Lane pointed.

Loraine pulled a tissue from her pocket and handed it to Lane. "Please?"

Lane wiped Ben's mouth with the tissue. The baby made a sucking motion while Lane cleaned up the mess on the tea towel.

Loraine took the tissue and threw it in a garbage can nearly full of lobster remains and newspaper. "Thanks." She looked over her shoulder. "I wouldn't want to upset Robert's sensitivities."

Lane laughed. *That must mean I don't have any!* he thought.

"No," Loraine read Lane's mind as she rubbed Ben's back, "I didn't mean it that way!" She laughed.

"Don't worry, I didn't take it that way." Lane looked at the lobster on his plate, wondering how Loraine could read his mind.

"How are Christine and Matt doing?" Loraine asked.

Lane shook his head, then gave Loraine a brief overview of the past month's events.

She listened without comment while patting Ben's back and rocking him whenever he fussed.

Arthur brought his chair over, creating an offset triangle as he listened to Lane's version of calamities and added any details Lane missed.

After they finished, Loraine smiled.

"I don't feel like smiling," Arthur said.

"Neither do I." Lane took another sip of beer.

"Christine is fighting back. Sure, you two and Matt are experiencing some collateral damage as a result. And yes, her father denies her existence. Still, she's with you, you're supporting her, she's found out she has a sister, and it sounds like she and Matt are acting like siblings usually act."

"This is normal?" Arthur's tone of voice revealed that

normal behaviour was not one of the conclusions he'd considered.

Loraine nodded. "About as normal as any other family."

Lane thought, *Family? People keep saying I've got a family.*

Arthur reached for the baby. Loraine handed him over.

"My turn next," Lane said.

Arthur and Loraine smiled at each other knowing that Lane would need to wait at least half an hour.

"Yes, and it's healthy when you think about it." Loraine read the doubtful expressions on the faces of Arthur and Lane. "I know that neither Matt nor Christine has had an easy life up until now, but their reactions and behaviours are to be expected. And," she paused for emphasis, "it looks like the two of you are supporting them just as you should by allowing them to have freedom and being there when they fall flat on their faces."

"It feels like we go from one disaster to another," Arthur said.

"Exactly. What else were you expecting?" Loraine reached into the cooler for a beer. She twisted off the top and took a sip while waiting for Lane or Arthur to say something.

Ben interrupted the conversation with a healthy fart. Then there were more sounds. The air between them filled with a ripe mixture of lobster, beer, butter, and baby shit.

Loraine smiled. "I think Ben just made an important point. There is always reality with kids. You have to expect hugs every so often, lobster not very often, and some crap every day." Loraine reached for the baby. "He needs a change."

Arthur said, "Allow me to change Ben."

"I'll help. We may never get another chance," Lane said.

Loraine smiled. "Go right ahead. Down the hall, last door on your right." She followed them into the living room where Lisa stood up to watch the proceedings.

Lane followed Arthur and Ben down the hall.

"Did you tell them what the paper cups are for?" Lisa asked Loraine.

"No." Loraine was halfway down the hall when the voices reached her.

"Cover him back up. It's like one of those fountains in Italy!" Arthur sounded close to panic.

"Sorry." Lane was laughing.

"I'm soaked!" Arthur began to laugh.

×

"Tell them about the door!" Matt said in between bites of pizza as they sat around the table on the deck in the shade cast by the neighbour's house.

Christine choked on her soft drink. Pop came out her nose. She reached for a napkin.

Lane handed her his.

Arthur patted her back.

Alexandra said, "You okay, baby?"

Christine nodded and wiped her nose.

Alex handed her another napkin.

"This is so embarrassing!" Christine said.

"Not as embarrassing as the door handle!" Matt laughed.

"What's the story about the door handle?" Arthur asked.

"We were downtown," Alexandra said.

"It was one of those big glass doors," Matt said.

Christine laughed. "Alex said, 'Here let me get this.' She pulled on this huge door handle, and it came off in her hand!"

"You should have seen the expression on the security guard's face when I handed it to him." Alexandra pantomimed a look of astonishment.

After they finished laughing, Arthur asked, "Where are you staying?"

Maybe this isn't a good idea, Lane thought.

"Downtown at a hotel," Alexandra reached for her glass.

"Why not stay with us? We've got room," Arthur said.

Christine got up, put her arms around Arthur's neck and hugged him.

Maybe it is, Lane thought.

×

"Madeline? Andrea? Where've my girls been?"

Maddy cringed at the sound of the woman's voice.

"Out." Maddy kicked her shoes off.

Andrea leaned closer to her sister and hugged Maddy's neck.

Maddy looked down the hall. Her mother sat up on the couch. She reached for a glass of wine, lifted it to her lips, and stuck her tongue inside of the glass. She managed to spill a drop on the front of her powder-blue tracksuit.

Maddy walked down the hall. She heard the sound of Andrea's sock feet on the hardwood.

"That doesn't tell us much," her stepfather said.

Maddy stepped into the front room. The windows reached two storeys. There was hardly a shadow in the room. Her stepfather stood with a full bottle of red wine in his left hand and a corkscrew in his right. She saw that he wore a white shirt and black slacks and was freshly shaved. His goatee was sharply defined.

"Well?" her stepfather asked.

Maddy thought, *Remember, anticipate the next question before answering.* "Out for lunch at the Mexican restaurant."

Her stepfather turned to his left. "Andrea?"

Andrea nodded. "Quesadillas."

"What kind?" He placed the opener over top the wine bottle and twisted the handle.

"Chicken." Andrea put her left hand in her sister's.

He looked at his daughter. "It's a big week for you, Andrea.

You're booked in for an appointment with me on Friday." He smiled and pulled at the cork.

Maddy felt her mouth watering and her stomach churning.

Mother held out her glass. "Top me up."

Maddy made it to the washroom with just enough time to lift the lid before watching undigested bits of corn and beans hurl into the toilet bowl.

chapter 14

Lane looked out from the second-storey terrace and down along Oxford Street. The trees on the sides of the street reached out limbs and budding leaves with a promise to obscure the view within weeks.

"So, you said we needed to begin from the beginning?" Harper sat across from Lane at a table just out the back door of the Kensington coffee shop. They were alone in the crisp morning air. Chattering birds seemed to make conversation all the more private.

"Back to the dentists, I think. The body had been cleaned up and wrapped. Fibre can't specify a cause of death. So we need to look at what leaves no trace. Fibre says it's likely nitrous oxide that was used to kill Jennifer." Lane sipped at his espresso mixed with chocolate and caramel.

"Remember how slow things were at the dentists' office? They're pulling up in their Mercedes, someone has spent a truckload of money decorating the place, and the office is empty. It doesn't add up."

"The waterfall," Lane said.

Harper put his cup down. "Pretty cryptic. Give me a bit more to go on."

"The waterfall in their office. It costs a fortune. How can they afford to have a lavish office, hire a staff, and pay for the equipment in a dentist's office?" Lane watched a blue jay as it squawked from its perch at the top of an evergreen tree.

Harper glanced at his laptop, pointed a finger at his notes, and read from the screen. "I've been checking into them. They've been partners for five years. Jones had his own practice for about seven years before that. Ever since he partnered with Stephen, their income has been pretty spectacular."

"So we're agreed that James Sanders is in the clear?" Lane asked.

"He couldn't have committed the crime since he was at the bar." Harper looked over the top of the screen.

"Agreed. What about the graffiti artist who appears to know so much about the crime?"

"We need to make another visit to Malcolm's, I think. Maybe he'll tell us more this time." Harper made a move to close the computer. "When are we going to stake out the back alley?" He looked down over the edge of the terrace at the alley running beneath them.

"Just a minute. Wasn't McTavish supposed to get back to us?"

Harper took his hand away from the laptop. "That's right."

"So, where do we start, again?" Lane said.

Lane's phone rang. He flipped it open. "Hello."

"I've got a woman calling long distance who claims she's your sister. She won't take no for an answer," the dispatcher said.

Lane thought, *My sister?* "Okay." Lane waited.

"Lane? Lane, is that you?"

"It's me." Lane felt tension grab him somewhere near his belt buckle.

"God knows! God knows!"

"God knows what?" Lane asked.

"God knows who, and what you are! God knows you just want to make sure you're in the will! God knows she set fire to that house!"

"Who is she?"

"Christine! I'm glad she's gone! That child has the mark of the devil on her! She's been too close to the fire!"

"Do you have any idea how ridiculous you sound, Allison?"
Enough of this! Lane thought.

Allison's words were saturated with sarcasm, indignation, and rage. "You! You're the one the family always jokes about! Laughs at what you do with that boyfriend of yours! You call me ridiculous! God knows who you are, and what you do! Don't you talk to me like that! God knows!"

Lane took the phone away from his ear.

"God knows!" Allison said.

He looked at the end button.

"God knows!"

He pressed it with his thumb, closed the phone, and looked around him.

Harper's eyes were wide. "Who was that?"

"My sister." Lane looked down at the dumpsters in the alley. "Do you think we should sit up here tonight?"

✕

"They're not in." Ramona sat behind the counter wearing a salmon top, salmon eyeshadow, and matching slacks.

Lane looked around the waiting room. Magazines were stacked neatly on two rosewood coffee tables. The fabric on the chairs was free of frays and snags.

"When are you expecting them back?" Harper asked.

"Tomorrow morning." Ramona glanced at the cover of the celebrity magazine. It was face down over her keyboard.

"What time?"

"By seven-thirty." Ramona looked at the phone as if willing it to ring.

✕

"So, what did Harry say when she phoned?" Lane asked.

Harper turned east off Centre Street and followed the road down an S curve. "Just said we should stop by. They have some information for us."

They parked between the open overhead doors. Once they had passed from sunlight into the shadow inside of Malcolm's shop, they could smell new paint, oil, and metal. They spotted vehicles in various stages of rebuilds, from rusted frames to a completely restored Beaumont in British racing green. The owner smiled from the driver's seat of the Beaumont. His grin grew wider when he turned the key.

"Five hundred horses!" Malcolm said over the growl of the engine. He closed the driver's door. "Take a spin. See how it feels."

The owner backed out into the parking lot. The tires chirped as he shifted into drive.

Malcolm smiled as the Beaumont rumbled. He looked at Lane and Harper. "Come on up to the office." Malcolm led the way past two nearly finished cars and one truck, then up the stairs at the back of the shop. He opened the door to the office and waited for the detectives to go in first.

Harry was on the phone, "Should be ready by tomorrow morning. Give me a call around nine and I'll give you an exact time. No problem." She hung up.

"They're here," Malcolm said.

Harry turned in her chair to face the detectives. "Hello."

She's cut her hair, Lane thought. "Looks good," he said.

Harry smiled.

"What looks good?" Malcolm asked.

"Harry's hair," Lane said.

Malcolm turned to his wife. "You got your hair cut?"

Harry's smile faded. "Yesterday."

Malcolm went to say something, thought better of it, and closed his mouth.

Harry said, "We've contacted a few people we know. No one knows who she is. The style used on the dumpsters is new."

"How do you know it's a she?" Harper asked.

"Intuition." Harry looked directly at Harper. "The 'W'

and the 'o'. A woman did this. It's about some kind of sexual assault. Some kind of exploitation."

"You sure?" Lane closed his eyes and recalled the image painted on Jennifer's dumpster. *Harry's probably right,* he thought.

Harry nodded, considered for a moment, and said, "Yes."

"What else?" Harper asked.

Malcolm looked at Harry. She waited. He took off his cap and said, "It looks like the artist only works one area: the back alleys of Kensington. No one has spotted her stuff anywhere else. And no one knows who she is. She's new."

"So?" Lane asked.

"So," Harry said, "if you want to find her, you know where to look. And now you know as much as we do."

"Except where to find Leo," Lane said.

Harry shook her head. "We've already told you all you need to know to find Leo."

"Thanks," Harper said.

Outside the shop, Lane and Harper looked at the cinder-block wall on the west side of the shop. It was a mosaic of multicoloured silhouetted artists in a variety of stylized poses, vintage vehicles in various stages of restoration, and tags.

Harper said, "Well, at least they've confirmed that we need to check out the alley."

"It's going to be a long night." Lane got into the Chev.

×

Lane walked in through the front door. Roz ran across the kitchen, barked once, saw him, wagged her tail, turned around, and skidded around the corner.

Lane followed and stood inside the open back door.

Alexandra and Christine talked across the table. Arthur used tongs to turn the burgers on the barbecue. Roz sat beside him, waiting for any morsels of fallen meat.

"Hello," Alexandra said. "Want some wine?"

"No thanks. I have to work late tonight. Just came home for supper." Lane smiled as Arthur turned to face him.

"Late shift?" Arthur asked.

"We need to nab an artist." Lane went back into the kitchen and poured himself a glass of water. His mouth tingled when he saw the salads waiting in the fridge. He went to throw a paper towel in the garbage and hesitated when he saw what was there.

Outside, Alexandra asked, "Artist?"

"Graffiti artist." Lane sat down and loosened his tie.

"I got caught tagging dumpsters in Kensington. Uncle Lane and I had to clean up, or I would have been charged. We found one dumpster with a tag on it and inside was a body. He wants to find whoever tagged the dumpster." Christine raised her eyebrows and sipped her pop.

Arthur turned around with his tongs pointed at the sky.

Alexandra watched Lane for his reaction.

"So, now you're a detective too?" Lane shook his head.

"Well, it isn't that difficult to figure out!" Christine looked to Arthur for support.

"Since we're solving mysteries, where did the money come from?" Lane asked.

"What money?" Alexandra adopted an innocent pose.

"The money that bought the new clothes and shoes." Lane watched the sisters look at one another, waiting to see who would answer first.

"Was it, by chance, your father's credit card?" Lane looked at Alexandra.

"Show-off. Do you always have to prove you're the master sleuth?" Christine crossed her arms across her chest. "You've been snooping through the garbage."

"Well, dad deserves to pay for the way he treated her," Alexandra said.

"How much?" Lane asked.

"He's got a twenty-five thousand dollar limit," Alexandra said.

"How much?" Lane asked.

"About two thousand," Christine said.

"Dollars?" Arthur asked.

"You bet." Alexandra lifted her wine glass.

"Feel any better?" Lane asked.

"I like the clothes." Christine smiled through her embarrassment.

"And the shoes. You've got some great shoe stores in this town." Alexandra swirled the wine around the inside of her glass.

Lane looked at Christine. "Do you feel any better?"

Christine shrugged. "Not really. You want me to take it all back?"

Alexandra said, "It's okay. Every time my dad had a fling and mom found out, she'd max out one of his credit cards. He'd always deny the fact that he was fooling around, then he would always pay the credit card bill without saying a word. It was understood. A family thing."

"This family works differently." Arthur turned to Christine. "No more running up the credit card bill."

✕

Maddy looked at the lock on her bedroom door. She looked at Andrea sleeping on the bed.

Maddy stood and walked from the desk to her sister. *Her skin is so soft,* she thought. Maddy brushed Andrea's cheek with the back of her hand.

Andrea pushed away the hand at her cheek. Her eyes opened.

"Go back to sleep. I'll wake you up later," Maddy said.

Andrea stuck a thumb in her mouth and nodded once.

×

Lane looked at the luminous dial on his watch. It was after one o'clock. He looked up the alley until he spotted the silhouette of Harper, who waved once.

Lane withdrew to the shadow running from the wall to the dumpster, where the streetlights weren't able to penetrate the night.

He sniffed the air, listened to a car driving along Kensington. Its tires hummed while its body slipped through the air. Across the river and downtown, he could hear a siren. It grew stronger, then weaker when it passed behind a building.

"Can we go home now? I'm tired."

It's the voice of a child, Lane thought.

"We're almost home."

A female. Definitely older than the first, Lane thought.

"Carry me."

Lane stepped from the shadow and into the muted light of the streetlight. He glanced sideways and coughed. Harper waved, then disappeared as he moved into a recessed doorway.

"Kind of late for a little one." Lane watched the older of the two. She was dressed in black. A piece of jewellery on one pierced ear glittered. She stopped. One hand held the little girl's and the other a black over-the-shoulder bag. *She's about as tall as I am and looks to be seventeen or eighteen,* Lane thought.

The little girl looked up at the older girl. "Who's he?"

"Don't know." The older girl put her hand inside her shoulder bag.

Lane reached for his ID. "I'm a detective with the city police."

"My little sister was at a sleepover. She started crying, so she phoned, and asked me to come and get her."

"I'm Detective Lane. The detective behind you is Harper."

Lane watched as the little one looked up at her older sister with a puzzled expression.

The older girl looked behind her as Harper moved into the middle of the alley about twenty metres away. She turned back to Lane. "So what?"

"So, we were hoping you'd introduce yourselves," Lane said.

"I don't think so." The older girl moved forward.

Lane heard the fear in her voice and noticed that the knee tremors affected the way she walked.

"What's the matter, Maddy?" the little girl said.

"Shh!" the older one said as she walked past Lane.

He turned to watch. They turned right and disappeared down Oxford Street.

Lane followed as far as the sidewalk, where he was able to observe their progress up the street.

Harper said, "Get a name?"

"The older one goes by Maddy."

They watched the pair cross the street, walk to the end of the block, and turn left.

"Hey, look at what's coming our way," Harper said.

Lane looked east. The man on the bicycle was coasting toward them. He braked at the corner and turned toward Kensington Road. At the side of the brick building, he stopped. Then the rider leaned on his left leg and used his right hand to lift his right leg over the seat. With two practised tugs on a bungee cord, he released the crutch attached to the bike's frame. He leaned over and reached into the saddlebag.

Lane thought, *You can't miss Leo. That's what Harry said. Of course, this has to be him. Hiding right under our noses!* He smiled.

Harper followed Lane, staying within the shadows.

They came upon Leo as he pulled out a can of spray paint and a Toblerone-sized marker from his saddlebag.

"Leo?" Lane asked.

Leo straightened, turned first to Lane, and then to Harper. "Good evening, officers."

Lane watched Leo. The man was sinew and bone. His clothes hung loose on his frame. His eyes were bright with intelligence. Leo's nose looked like it belonged to a bird. He was balancing on one foot because the withered right leg was several centimetres shorter than the left. The crutch was a couple of centimetres off the ground so that he could balance on his good leg.

He's ready for a fight if it comes to that, Lane thought.

"We're here for information, not to make an arrest," Harper said.

Leo smiled, "I take it that if I tell you what you want to know, then I go free. If I don't, I get arrested. Have I read the subtext correctly?" He turned his back to the wall so that he could watch both detectives at the same time.

Lane moved closer to Harper. *This way we're less of a threat because he has an avenue for escape.*

A puzzled expression appeared on Leo's face, then disappeared.

Harper leaned against the wall. The sound of tires on pavement passed, then hummed west along Kensington Road.

"Someone tagged a dumpster just down the alley. The tag identified the body of the person inside. We're trying to find the artist." Lane leaned against a transformer.

Leo studied the concrete at his feet. "What does that have to do with me?"

"We've checked around. You're known to be the resident artist. We thought you might know some of the others who work this area," Harper said.

"People do stuff for their own reasons. I don't know why that dumpster was painted the way it was. And that's all I can tell you." Leo leaned on his crutch.

"We're trying to catch a murderer. The victim was in her mid-twenties," Harper said.

"Are you accusing me?" Leo asked.

"Are you guilty?" Lane thought, *Don't play games with me!*

Leo smiled. "Not of murder, but I am guilty of graffiti."

×

Maddy doubled back down the alley, turned left at their garage, and approached the back door.

She noted the pale blue light from the TV. Maddy reached into her pocket after putting her index finger to her lips. Andrea mimed the warning. The key slid easily into the lock. Maddy kept the lock lubricated with graphite just for nights like this. Maddy held her breath and opened the door. The muted sound of voices on the TV reached down the hall. In the living room, light flickered and faded on the wall.

Her mother lay on the floor in a puddle of bloody vomit. It looked to Maddy as if her mother's hair had stuck to the drying mess.

"Mom?" Andrea said.

Maddy leaned over to check for a pulse at her mother's neck. She held her breath and thought, *There's something there!*

"Mom!" Andrea said.

Maddy's mind raced. *Get Andrea out of here!* "Andrea. Go to the kitchen and run a cloth under the tap. I'll come and get it! You stay there."

Andrea scampered down the hall and turned on the light in the kitchen.

Maddy looked around her, reached for the phone, and dialed 911.

chapter 15

"We've got another message." Harper's phone voice sounded rough at ten o'clock in the morning.

Lane opened one eye to see the shaft of light peeking between the curtains. "How'd we miss it? What's it say?"

"It was across the street from where we were. It says, 'Jennifer wasn't the first. She won't be the last'."

Lane sat up in bed. "Is Fibre on it?"

"There already. There's something else."

Lane's feet touched the floor. He rubbed his face with his free hand. *Think!*

"That ambulance we saw last night. I checked the address. The house belongs to a Dr. Joseph Jones. His wife was taken to the hospital. I made some calls, and she's in detox for at least a week."

"The same Dr. Jones?"

"That's right, and he has two daughters. One is seventeen. The other is five."

"Is one of them named Maddy?" Lane asked.

"Madeline is the oldest and Andrea the youngest."

Lane thought, *This is way too close to home to be one big coincidence!*

✕

"Detective Lane?"

Lane adjusted the cell phone against his ear. "That's right."

"Chief Smoke here. Any updates?"

Lane hesitated. "We're in the process of checking out several promising leads."

"Good! Your work in the past has been exemplary. So

many high-profile cases solved. You're an asset to our police force and the community."

"Thank you, sir." *It sounds like he's slurring his words. He can't be drunk before lunch*, Lane thought.

The chief cleared his throat. "There's a promotion in the works, and your name is at the top of my list when this case is wrapped up."

I wonder what you'll say when you find out a drinking buddy of yours is a suspect, Lane thought.

"Just remember, this case is your priority. Get back to me with any new developments." The chief hung up.

That's one order I don't think I'll be able to follow, Lane thought.

×

"Is Mom okay? Can we go visit her?" Andrea wore a pink jacket, pink shoes, pink pants, and matching backpack. She'd insisted on the outfit. She held tightly to Maddy's hand.

"Not for a while." Maddy looked across the open field as they approached Andrea's elementary school, which was situated next to Maddy's high school.

"Why?" Andrea looked up at her big sister.

"She's sick."

"Booze and pills. Booze and pills." Andrea sang it.

Maddy stopped, crouched down, and looked her little sister in the eye. "Please don't sing that at school." *All we need is another rumour going around.*

Andrea shook her head, looking very adult for an instant. "Okay."

After getting Andrea to school, Maddy entered her school through the door near the parking lot under the library. She walked down an empty hallway and past the office, looking neither right as she hatched an excuse for being late for English class.

"Madeline?"

She continued on, cursing under her breath, hoping to make it to the stairs. *I should have been listening to music!* she thought.

"Madeline?"

She turned as a hand tapped her on the shoulder. "Yes?"

Ms. McMurphy, who was a head shorter than Maddy, smiled beneath her mustache. "Got a minute?"

"Actually, I'm late for English." Maddy cocked a thumb over her shoulder.

Ms. McMurphy gestured for Maddy to follow. "Don't worry. I'll give you a note for being late."

Maddy followed her into the main office and into McMurphy's office. The assistant principal waited for Maddy to sit down at a round table before shutting the door.

McMurphy smiled and sat down across from Maddy.

Half the west wall was windows. Maddy closed her eyes, feeling the sunlight on her face.

"I pulled your file. Very impressive. Honours average. Your teachers rave about your work."

Maddy yawned and looked out the window.

"Still, I'm worried," McMurphy said.

Maddy shrugged. *It's best not to say anything. If you say anything, it's like opening a door. Once she's in there, who knows what she'll find out.* Maddy felt sweat gathering along her hairline and under her arms. She crossed her legs.

"You do very well. And yes, I heard about what happened in guidance. I also heard about the ambulance."

Maddy felt rage shake her. "That's none of your damned business! Just like it was none of his damned business! How can you have someone like him working in a school? How do you think he found out about those pictures?"

McMurphy's face was a mask. She waited.

Maddy sat back. *There, you did it. You opened the door! Fool!*

"I've heard about the pictures, too. Can we talk about them?"

Maddy closed her mouth and her mind, to allow her to go where she always went at times like these. To the beach in Mexico where her mother played with her in the waves. Where they were safe. Where they laughed. Where her mother was sober.

"And you take care of your little sister. She's devoted to you and you to her, but..."

Don't complete her sentence for her! Maddy thought.

McMurphy smiled.

Don't open your mouth!

McMurphy crossed her legs.

It's a trap!

McMurphy looked at her fingernails.

What if I can't stop what's planned for Friday? "My mom is in detox for at least a week. My dad never came home last night. Who else is there to take care of Andrea?"

McMurphy didn't blink, didn't look away, and waited.

Maddy thought, *Didn't you hear what I just said? Keep your mouth shut!* Rage curled up and swelled inside of her. It rolled over top of her defenses to crash over every other thought, every other emotion. She held her hand over her mouth, stood, opened the door to McMurphy's office, stepped through the door and slammed it. Glass rattled up and down the corridor. The secretaries looked up, startled, and, Maddy realized, a bit afraid.

✕

"Detective Lane?"

Lane didn't recognize the voice on his cell phone. He glanced at Harper who was negotiating the car through road construction. "That's correct."

"It's Leo. Remember?"

Lane took the phone away from his ear, looked at call display, memorized the number, and said, "I remember."

"I thought about what you said."

"And?"

Harper slowed the car and stopped behind a cement truck.

Leo said, "Be on the lookout for two sisters."

"Could you give me just a bit more to go on? The quicker we can finish this, the less chance there is that someone else will be hurt."

There was quiet for a full thirty seconds. "One is in high school, and the other in kindergarten. They live close by. Things aren't as perfect as they seem."

The connection ended.

×

"How's your wife?" Lane sat across from Doctor Joseph Jones in his back-room office. Lane sensed Harper was waiting to ask a few questions of his own.

"My wife?" Dr. Jones looked only slightly more puzzled than he'd been when they walked through the empty waiting room past a dozing Ramona and into his office.

"Yes, your wife," Harper said.

Lane thought, *Harper's angry, and when he's angry his questions often tip the suspect off balance. Let's see how it will work this time.*

"She's at home." The doctor leaned back and smiled as if he'd just got the joke.

Harper's anger cut its way into the pauses between the words. "It's our understanding that she's in detox after an ambulance rushed her to emergency late last night."

"That's impossible," Dr. Jones said.

"Impossible or not, she's been admitted." Harper leaned his hands on Jones' desk. "Where were you last night, then?"

Jones' cheeks and ears flushed red. He looked over Lane's

shoulder at the door, then out the window as if measuring the distance.

"It's a simple question, Mr. Jones," Lane said.

The door opened. Lane and Harper turned. Dr. Paul Stephen stood in the doorway.

Lane watched as Stephen made eye contact with Jones. Both dentists wore neatly trimmed goatees and designer labels. But there was something different in Stephen's blue eyes. Lane felt he was in the company of a salesman about to begin working the room, putting a spin on the facts.

"Did you want me to join the meeting?" Dr. Stephen asked.

"Not at this time," Harper said.

"Yes!" Jones began to stand up but was stopped by a glare from Stephen. "The detectives are trying to find out what happened to Ms. Towers."

"You're still looking for the murderer?" Dr. Stephen asked.

Lane heard the sarcasm in Stephen's voice, but ignored the implied superiority, the suggestion that the detectives could be doing a better job. "That's correct."

"We had nothing to do with that. Her boyfriend, however, was quite unpredictable. It is in our best interests for you to quickly bring the person responsible to justice." Stephen crossed his arms and leaned against the door jam.

Harper shifted in his seat to get a better look at the second dentist. "Jennifer's boyfriend has an alibi."

"There must be some mistake!" Jones looked at Harper and worked at keeping his composure. "Jennifer was often fearful of her boyfriend. And, in confidence, she said as much to both of us." The dentist looked at his partner.

Dr. Stephen nodded. "Yes, she was quite fearful of him."

How come Stephen's tone of voice and posture have shifted? Lane thought.

"There's no mistake about the alibi. The witness is quite

certain. That's why we're back here talking with you two." Harper smiled at Stephen.

Lane thought, *It's remarkable how alike the doctors look. I wonder who imitates who?* Then he looked at the family portrait on the shelf to one side of Jones' desk. He hid his recognition of the daughters in the photo.

Jones' voice allowed condescension to creep into his voice. "We all know that witnesses are notoriously unreliable. Might I suggest that you also check the credentials of this witness who provided such a questionable alibi?"

×

Lane's phone rang as they drove east along Crowchild Trail.

"Hello."

"Dr. Weaver here."

Lane glanced at Harper and mouthed, "Fibre." Harper nodded.

"Good morning," Lane said.

"I am still unable to determine the exact cause of death, which continues to be an indicator in and of itself." Fibre spoke with his patented toneless delivery.

Lane looked across at the LRT cars traveling at the same speed as their Chev. One male passenger looked down on them from a superior height. The train gently swayed. The man closed his eyes.

"Nitrous oxide leaves the body very quickly and is difficult to trace. Numerous avenues have been explored to determine the exact precursor to Ms. Tower's death, but the only certainties are unconsciousness, suffocation, and death. Nitrous oxide, resulting in unconsciousness, is a working theory fitting the outcome. All other reasonable conclusions have been entirely eliminated," Fibre said.

Lane waited, watched the LRT slow for Dalhousie Station. "Anything on the most recent message from Kensington?"

"The paint matches the samples taken from the others. The style also suggests it was done by the same individual."

"Thanks," Lane said.

"Anything else I can do?" There was emotion in Fibre's voice.

Ever since he insulted my niece, Fibre can't do enough for us. "If I think of anything, you'll be the first to know."

"Good. And about your niece…" Fibre began, hesitated, and then hung up.

A change in tone is something Fibre's never done before. I may have been wrong about him. Maybe he does have feelings. Lane closed his phone.

"What's up?" Harper asked.

"Fibre still thinks Jennifer died from an overdose of nitrous oxide, but can't prove it." Lane tucked the phone in his pocket.

"So, we know where to keep looking."

"Head into Kensington. Do you have the home address for Jones?" Lane asked.

×

Maddy adjusted the book bag on her shoulder. *It's nice having one class off.* She savoured the unaccustomed freedom while sniffing the back alley mélange of garbage and tantalizing odours exhaled through restaurant kitchen fans. She turned left out of the alley and onto Oxford Street.

Ahead, two men in sports coats and black shoes got out of a grey four-door Chevrolet. The driver wore a mustache and was taller than the other one, who exited from the passenger side. The passenger adjusted something on his hip.

"Shit!" Maddy recognized the shorter detective from the other night in the alley. She stepped behind a shrub on the boulevard, then leaned to look around it. Her nose filled with the purple-sweet scent of lilacs.

The officers looked down the sidewalk and past her. One pointed at something above and behind Maddy. She looked over her shoulder, and saw the terrace of the coffee shop.

They turned to walk to the front door of her house. She waited until they returned to the car. She heard the engine start and realized they would spot her if they drove to the end of the street to turn around.

The car moved toward her.

She stepped sideways to keep the budding foliage between her and the unmarked police car.

As the car moved across from her, she looked through the bush and inside the car. The detective who had talked with her the other night was looking directly at her.

She ran back down the sidewalk, through the green metal gate, and down the alley.

Maddy heard the scrubbing sound of tires stopping suddenly. A car door slammed. Running footsteps followed her. The car engine roared and receded.

She ran down the alley, through a parking lot and, without looking for traffic, across Kensington Road. The driver of a white pickup truck sounded his horn and hit the brakes. The truck's rear wheels locked. It skidded sideways in a howl of off-road rubber.

Maddy held onto her book bag with her right hand and pushed off from the truck's hood with her left. She sprinted east, then took a sharp right toward the river. Behind her, she heard the wail of a siren.

×

Lane skidded on a patch of pea-sized gravel when he rounded the corner of the parking lot. After getting his feet back under him, he heard the pickup truck lock its brakes and skid. Lane checked left and right before stepping between two cars and onto Kensington Road. His attention was focused on Maddy.

He was certain she would fall under the truck's front wheels. Instead, she used her left arm to push off from the truck and sidestep nimbly across the street. He watched her dance away as he stepped out into traffic.

The truck's momentum carried it forward. Lane and the truck promptly ran into one another. Lane found himself bouncing off the truck's front fender before being thrown with a thump into the side of a parked car. He lay there, next to the truck's exhaust pipe, inhaling its fumes, and thought, *My feet are okay, my ankles and my calves.*

A siren wailed. Brakes screamed.

My legs? Nothing broken there.

"Buddy, you okay?" someone asked.

"Lane!"

Fingers? Yes, they're moving just fine. Lane flexed them just to make sure. *That's strange. My left hand is tingling.*

"Lane? Are you all right?"

Lane turned his head, feeling no stiffness in his neck. He opened his eyes. *I know those shoes.*

"Lane?"

The familiar black shoes became knees and then a face with its left cheek flattened by the pavement.

"What are you doing there?" Lane asked.

"Are you okay?" Harper asked.

Lane wiggled the fingers of his left hand. "Are they moving?"

Harper looked at the hand. "Yes, they're working."

"How the hell did the cops get here so fast?" someone asked.

Who's that? Lane thought.

Harper looked over his shoulder to talk to the driver of the truck. "He's my partner."

"Oh," the voice said.

"Shut off the engine! Christ, we're gonna suffocate here!"

Harper said.

This is very strange. Lane tried to sit up.

"Stay still." Harper put his hand on Lane's shoulder.

"I feel fine," Lane said.

"I'm calling an ambulance." Harper held his partner down with his left hand. With his right, he pressed three buttons on a cell phone. "You're not moving 'til it gets here."

×

Maddy doubled back. She saw the traffic lined up along either side of Kensington Road. Further east, she saw the flashing lights of a police cruiser. She waited to cross at the crosswalk. An ambulance and a blue and white police car howled down the back alley to get to the scene.

In five minutes she was back home. As she opened the back door, Lane's card fell from where it had been wedged between the door and the jamb. She picked up the card and stuffed it her bag. Then she found her mother's credit cards and the keys to the Mercedes.

×

"Whoaaaaaaaa!" The cry came from the woman in the adjacent bed in the emergency room.

She must be drying out, Lane thought. He stared at the ceiling. His left elbow throbbed, keeping time to the beat of his heart.

"Watch out!" the woman said.

Lane looked at the curtain separating them. The woman sat up. A silhouette appeared against the blue fabric.

"Hey baby!"

Lane thought, *This is worse than being hit by the truck.* The curtain bulged toward him as the woman pawed at it.

"Look out for the train!" The woman shadowboxed with the curtain separating them.

"Uncle?" Christine asked.

Lane looked at the faces at the foot of the bed. Christine had been crying. Arthur looked like someone other than Roz had crapped in his garden. Alexandra stood back with a puzzled expression.

Harper came up behind them. "Reinforcements have arrived. The good news is nothing's broken and the truck sustained minor damage. The better news is Lane's supposed to take the rest of the week off."

Arthur asked, "Really?"

The woman in the next bed said, "Fat chance!"

"Where's Matt?" Lane asked.

"He's been suspended. I have to go there next," Arthur said.

"Smith is threatening to kick him out of the play," Christine said.

Lane closed his eyes. Even his eyelids were beginning to feel bruised. He said, "I'm going with you."

×

The Mercedes' tires scrubbed against the curb. Maddy pulled the wheel to the left 'til the sound stopped. She dropped the sedan into park and shut the engine off. The car rocked back and forth a couple of times. Maddy looked to her right at the playground and parking lot. She opened the door, stepped out, and looked into the back seat, where Andrea's clothes and favourite stuffed animals gazed vacantly back at her.

Maddy fiddled with the key until the doors locked. She looked across the parking lot to the front of the school, where buses and various other vehicles waited to pick up children. She walked through the front door of the school, rehearsing what she was going to say.

"Good afternoon, Madeline."

Maddy looked up. The principal and Maddy's stepfather

stood side by side. Both gave their best impressions of a TV guru's self-help smile.

"Hello." Maddy managed a smile. "So, this is a surprise." She played the game of artificial bonhomie that her family played at relatives' houses, parent-teacher interviews, and surprise meetings like this one.

The principal, a fiftyish woman who always wore a skirt, pashmina scarf, and vest said, "Here comes Andrea."

"I've come to take you both out for dinner." Jones smiled to reveal all of his carefully whitened front teeth.

"What great news, Daddy!" Maddy was unsuccessful at hiding her sarcasm. Dr. Jones grabbed her elbow.

He turned to the principal. "Thank you." He took Andrea's hand, and led the way out and down the front steps.

"Where are we going?" Maddy asked.

"It's a surprise," her stepfather said.

×

Lane recognized the emotion behind Matt's eyes. His nephew sat in a chair in the main office.

Lane thought, *You figure you're beat, again. When will you start to believe that we'll stick by you?* "What happened?" he asked.

The secretary glanced at them from behind her desk and computer.

Matt shook his head. "One of the grade tens was being beaten up. A grade eleven head-butted him into the chain link fence. Another kicked him when he fell to the ground."

"Where is he?" Arthur sat down on the other side.

"His parents came and took him to the hospital. It looks like he broke some ribs." Matt looked at the clock on the wall with a thousand-metre stare. "I'm missing rehearsal. Smith says I'm gonna be suspended. So I won't be in the play."

Lane almost said, *What did you do?* Instead he said, "How were you involved?"

"I picked the kid up off the ground. Mr. Smith came along and suspended us all because he said we were fighting." Matt shrugged.

Lane looked at Arthur, who nodded, indicating Lane should continue the conversation. "How did it start?"

"The kid was wearing a pink sweater." Matt turned to look at Lane.

"And you helped him up?" Arthur asked.

"Yep," Matt said.

"How come you got involved?" Lane asked.

"They were calling the kid a fag. It made me mad."

Lane heard the sharp intake of Arthur's breath. He stood up and walked over to the secretary. "We would like to see the principal, please."

The secretary smiled. "I'll see if he's available."

The door to the office swung open, banged against the wall, rebounded, and hit the back of a hard-shelled orange costume with black dots. A voice came from somewhere inside the black insect head of the costume. "I wanna see the principal!" One of the ladybug's gloved black hands had a young man by the arm. The boy was dressed in a blue nylon jacket. His look of pure bewilderment was accented by his unruly red hair.

"Hey, Fergus," Matt said.

Fergus looked in Matt's direction and gave a quick wave before being dragged up to the secretary's desk.

The bug said, "I'm tired of being assaulted by kids from this school. They think it's funny to shove me on my back and watch me try to get back up!"

"You work for the flower shop across the street?" the secretary asked.

"That's right. I work for Ladybug's Flowers," the voice said.

The secretary said, "You're next after them." She nodded in the direction of Lane, Arthur, and Matt.

Lane looked closely at the bug, which appeared to be over nine feet tall. One of the black dots on the ladybug's chest, near the neck, was made of a fine mesh. A pair of eyes, a nose, and a mustache were visible behind the mesh.

"Mr. Lane and Mr. Merali, how are you?" Fergus asked as he pulled free of the ladybug and sat down one seat away from Lane. The ladybug perched on the edge of a chair on the far side of Fergus.

Arthur took a deep breath. "In a bit of a predicament, I'm afraid."

Fergus smiled and cocked his head in the direction of the ladybug. "Me too."

Lane began to laugh, followed by Matt and the secretary.

The bug said, "What's so damned funny? This is serious!"

Arthur looked at Fergus' quizzical expression and began to laugh.

"This isn't funny!" The ladybug roared.

Lane's ribs and back ached, but he couldn't stop laughing.

"Hello." A hand appeared in front of Lane's face. Lane looked up to see the hand was attached to a slender man of over six feet who had a smile and full head of blond hair. "Jim Baldwin."

"Lane. This is Arthur and Matt." Lane watched the principal shake their hands.

"I hear great things about your performance in the upcoming play," Baldwin said as he shook hands with Matt. "Let's talk." Baldwin led them into his office, where he closed the door behind them.

They all sat around a table across from Baldwin's desk.

Matt put his hands palms down on the tabletop.

Arthur said, "Matt defended a student who was being assaulted for wearing a pink sweater. Now he's being threatened with missing the play."

Baldwin looked at each of them in turn.

Lane watched the man's eyes as they studied the backs of Matt's hands.

No contusions, Lane thought.

Baldwin looked at Matt's face.

No marks there.

"Our nephew stepped in to help another student and is being punished. Please help me to understand the reasoning behind that decision." Arthur looked at Lane to see if he had anything to add.

"I've just been made aware of the situation." Baldwin watched Lane. "Four students were suspended for fighting."

Arthur said, "No problem there — but only if Matt was, in fact, fighting. And I have another question."

Baldwin turned to Arthur.

"Why is our nephew being threatened and bullied for defending another student? Especially in an assault that looks like it was motivated by bigotry?" Arthur's eyes zeroed in on Baldwin. "Also, Mr. Smith has a history of bullying our nephew, and it's time for that to stop."

Lane remembered their last meeting with Smith, and the teacher's arrogant sarcasm.

The principal waited a moment before picking up the phone and dialing four numbers. "Mr. Smith? I have Matt, one of the students suspended, and his uncles here. Please join us."

Baldwin hung up the phone, stood up, and opened the door.

Lane took a long breath and looked at Matt, who said, "I told you it would never be over."

Arthur took the offensive before Baldwin could shut the door or Smith (wearing a crisp navy blue suit and tie) could sit down. "Why is our nephew being suspended for defending another student? I'm sure the school board does not condone gay bashing."

Baldwin sat down.

Smith sat down next to him.

Lane watched a faux smile spread across Smith's narrow face. Smith said, "We have a zero-tolerance policy when it comes to fighting. Your nephew was involved, so he was suspended." Smith kept his voice low, its tone sweetened with artificial sincerity.

You remember us, and we remember you Mr. Smith, Lane thought. "Is there any physical evidence to support your theory?"

Smith looked surprised. "Physical evidence?"

"Marks on Matt's face or hands would be physical evidence that he was involved in a fight." Lane studied Baldwin, who studied him in turn.

"Ummm…" Smith said.

"I don't like it when someone bullies our nephew. And this is not the first time this has happened, Mr. Smith," Arthur said.

"It's policy." Smith glanced at Baldwin.

"So, it's policy for you to bully and threaten our nephew? To threaten him with expulsion when he went to the aid of another student who was being bullied?" Arthur's tone was low and his face was red.

Baldwin stood up. "Could I please have a phone number I can reach you at?"

Lane reached into his pocket, winced at his sore muscles and pulled out his card. "Could I borrow a pen, please?"

Baldwin handed him one.

Lane wrote his cell phone number on the back of the card and handed it, and the pen, to the principal.

Baldwin looked at the card and shook hands with Lane, Arthur, and Matt. "I'll get back to you before this evening is over."

×

Lane answered his cell phone as Arthur drove home along John Laurie Boulevard. "Hello?"

"Jim Baldwin here. Matt's drama teacher expects him at rehearsal tomorrow night. I explained why your nephew missed rehearsal this evening. I apologize for our mistake."

Lane tried to look at his nephew and found he couldn't turn his neck. "Thank you."

"Please ask Matt to come by and see me at eight-thirty tomorrow morning so that I can thank him for coming to the assistance of the student who was being assaulted," Baldwin said.

"Thank you for getting back to us so quickly," Lane said.

"We were lucky," Baldwin said.

"How's that?" Lane asked.

"We had two independent witnesses," Baldwin said.

"The ladybug and Fergus?" Lane asked.

"That's right." Baldwin laughed and broke the connection.

×

Lane woke at three a.m. Somehow, the nightmare he had just had made the air seem thicker. He could see the child's body in the garbage can. He could see the dead child in the back of the camper. He could see Jennifer's body in the dumpster. And he could smell death.

chapter 16

"We're going with you." Matt sat outside Kuldeep's coffee shop. He'd insisted on stopping with Lane and Roz for an early morning cup of coffee.

Lane sat back very slowly, looked at Roz who sat with her legs tucked to one side while she watched their conversation. He looked through the glass at the people who filled the tables inside the coffee shop. *I don't know if you should, Matt. You don't know what you'll be dealing with.*

"You think you're protecting us, but there's a difference between sheltering and protecting." Matt looked over his shoulder at Roz. "We're all strays. You, Arthur, Christine, and me. You think we don't know how harsh things can be?"

Lane put his cup down. He eased his head back, expecting pain. He wasn't disappointed. "I don't want them to do to you what they did to me. You've been through enough — so has Christine, and so has Arthur."

"You've got it all wrong. This isn't about us. You and Uncle Arthur stuck with me yesterday, now we're going to stick with you." Matt pointed at Lane and took a pull from his bottle of orange juice.

Lane looked at the chocolate sprinkles floating on top of the melted whipped cream. He felt the aches in his body that were just beginning to reveal themselves.

Matt put his drink down. "You need to say goodbye to your dad, just like I needed to say goodbye to my mom. And I'm gonna be there for you, just like you were there for me."

Lane started to say something, but stopped. *What do I say, Matt?*

"Are you and Uncle Arthur gonna split up?" Matt asked.

"Where did that come from?"

Matt peeled the label from the bottle of orange juice. "Ever since Christine came along, things have been so tense. I thought..."

"You thought?" Lane asked.

Matt shrugged. "I don't know. I just thought with all of the stress, you two might, you know." He looked at Lane, then looked away. "We were becoming a family, then she came along. Now everyone's always fighting."

"It's been hard, yes, but it's also been..." Lane searched for the right word.

"Well?" Matt looked at Roz, who seemed to be expecting an answer too.

"Interesting. It's been interesting," Lane said. "Anything else?"

"Will you come to my play?" Matt asked.

"Yes."

"Promise?" Matt asked.

"Promise. Now I'd better get you to school."

"As long as you pick me up at eleven-thirty so I can go with you to the funeral," Matt said.

"Deal."

Four hours later, Lane came downstairs, where everyone, including Alexandra, waited in the front room. He scanned their outfits. Arthur slid back a cufflinked sleeve, tapped his watch, and said, "We've got to go and pick up Matt."

After picking up Matt, the drive downtown was quiet. Arthur found a place to park at the back of the cathedral between the Elbow River and Seventeenth Avenue. They walked around the church and past the old railway station, which was now home to a ballet studio. Lane looked over his shoulder at the bridge where one of his classmates had jumped into the river on a dare.

Matt held one of the massive wooden cathedral doors open for them. Inside, the scents of wood, wool, perfume, and incense pushed Lane back more than thirty years as he recalled leaning against his father's shoulder during a particularly lengthy summer sermon. He looked up and saw the sun playing with suspended bits of dust just as it had more than three decades ago. The light was all of the colours of stained glass, adding ripe shading to the textures of wood and metal.

"Family?" the usher asked. He wore a black jacket, grey wool slacks, and an obligatory smile.

"Not any more," Christine muttered.

"We'll sit at the back, thank you." Lane took Christine's arm and led them to the last pew.

Lane waited for the four to file past him and slide down the pew before he sat nearest the aisle and next to Christine. He studied the backs of heads to see if he recognized anyone. The congregation was a mix of well-to-do oilmen, lawyers, businessmen, and their families. *Dad always was well connected,* he thought.

The mass began with a hymn. Lane scrambled for a hymnal and the correct words.

After a series of prayers and hymns, one of the altar boys brought out the incense and handed it to the priest. Lane watched the incense rise to form a layer of smoke above their heads. The light from the stained glass windows changed as it passed through the smoke.

When Lane inhaled the scent, he remembered his father. The smell of his pipe tobacco. The feel of his wool suit against Lane's face. There was the memory of an embrace as his father's arm wrapped around Lane's shoulders. Lane remembered falling asleep and waking when his father gently shook him at the end of a mass.

The bishop stood atop three steps in front of the altar.

His hair brushed the belly of the smoke that was sprawled like a tired dog.

Bishop Paul began the eulogy.

Lane thought, *It's a bit unusual for the bishop to do this. No, of course he'd do this. He wants to make an impression on this crowd.*

The bishop wore the flowing, angelic robes of his office. He raised his arms to direct his flock, "Martin Lane was baptized in this church, lived his life as a loyal follower of Christ, and remained that way through the many trials life sent his way. In the last few years, he often spoke to me of these trials, and how they tested his faith. Ultimately, Martin remained faithful to the church despite these tests of faith."

Lane looked to his right. Christine's hands were shaking. She held them between her knees.

"Christine?" Lane asked.

She stared at her hands as if willing them to be still.

"We can learn a valuable lesson from Martin Lane's life. He refused to compromise his beliefs. He did this despite the tremendous challenge that comes with following the laws of the church in these times," the bishop said.

Lane looked up, knowing where the sermon was headed.

Christine leaned against him. "It's all the same. No matter what church I go to, it's all the same," she said.

"Those who remain faithful to the church and its teachings must look to the word of God. If we remain true to his teachings, we will find ourselves in paradise." Paul lifted a bible as a visual aid.

Christine wrapped her arms around her ribs and shivered. "It's all the same. Just like Paradise. He's just the same as Whitemore. You and I will never be good enough."

"God's path to redemption is not easy. And Martin Lane chose God's path for his family and, as a faithful follower of the church, he could not condone sin." Bishop Paul looked at Lane. "Even though Martin forgave the sinner, he could not forgive the sin!"

Christine began to sob. "Is this what they did to you?" She looked up at Lane. "Paradise did it to me too." Tears rolled down her face. She wiped a sleeve across her upper lip.

Lane handed her a handkerchief, stood up, looked directly back at the bishop, leaned down to help Christine stand, and led her down the aisle. He and his niece walked to the door.

When the door closed behind the five of them, Lane looked around at the trees and their fresh green buds. A pair of robins sang to each other.

Christine leaned against him, "I'm sorry uncle. It just brought back too many bad memories."

Lane smiled. "Don't worry about it. You helped make it clear to me for the first time why I was right to leave that life."

Christine hooked her arm in his and hugged his shoulder. Then she embraced Alex.

Lane felt Matt's hand on his back.

Arthur put his open palm on Lane's cheek and used his handkerchief to wipe the tears from Christine's face.

They walked back to the old railway bridge, leaned on the railing, and spent ten minutes watching the sparkling river flow beneath their feet.

✕

Lane got the phone call on the way back from the funeral.

"Detective?"

Lane recognized the voice. "Leo?"

"That's right. You'd better take a look over at Oxford Street. Find the biggest, fanciest house there. Both of the girls you are looking for were picked up at their school yesterday."

"Who picked them up?" Lane asked.

"Their father."

"Thanks, Leo," Lane said.

×

Erinn opened the back door. Jessica peeked out from between her mother's knees. When she saw Lane, she frowned and sucked her thumb. Mother and daughter wore T-shirts and sweatpants that matched their red hair. "How are you feeling?" Erinn held the door open.

If I tell her that every part of my body aches, she'll tell Arthur, Lane thought. "Fine," he said.

"Liar. Want a coffee? Cam's still in the shower." Erinn turned. Jessica ran into the kitchen.

Lane sat down at the kitchen table. He closed his eyes at the pain and smiled. He savoured the words of support from Matt, Christine, Arthur, and even Alexandra. Lane thought, *I've got my own family to worry about now.*

Erinn put a cup of coffee in front of him. "I'll get you some painkillers."

Lane smiled. "Who's the detective now?"

The bathroom door opened and Harper stepped out. Jessica ran down the hallway.

Erinn frowned. "You two don't know what you do to us every time one of you gets hurt."

"I don't mean it to happen." Lane opened the bottle of painkillers she set in front of him.

"Take two." Erinn sat down with a fresh cup of coffee. "I know you don't mean it to happen, but it keeps happening."

"Christine was really angry with me last night." Lane took two pills and chased them with coffee. "So was Matt."

"And Arthur?"

Lane looked at her. "Furious."

Erinn looked at him and shook her head. "For a smart guy, I'm amazed you haven't figured it out yet."

Lane felt a pang of emotion grab him unexpectedly by the throat.

"You're a family. The four of you. Or is it five now?" Erinn smiled mischievously.

How come I just figured it out and you knew already? Lane thought. *Is this how families act?* "I'm just figuring it out."

"That's the problem. You can figure out other people but not yourself. A niece and a nephew move in. What's it been? One year or two?" Erinn stood up, grabbed the pills, and put them in the cupboard above the fridge.

"It's hard to get my head around it. I just never expected us to have a family. Just another thing we couldn't expect in our lives. Now they're here, and I don't know what to make of it." Lane studied the concentric circles in the coffee in his cup. He looked up.

Harper stood with Jessica nestled at his throat. Both were watching Lane and Erinn.

"Where's Glenn?" Lane asked.

"University. Got an exam today," Harper said.

"We've got to go and find Maddy's school," Lane said.

"How come you're not taking time off?" Harper asked.

"Because whoever did the graffiti, and it's looking more and more like it was Maddy, is becoming more desperate." Lane grimaced as he leaned back into the chair.

"And you'll be able to chase her down if we find her?" Harper asked.

Lane smiled. "No. I'll leave the legwork to you. And…" he looked at Erinn, "I'll have Cam's back."

Forty minutes later, they parked in the visitors' parking on the gravel lot behind Maddy's school. Harper got out and waited for Lane to ease out of the passenger's side.

They stood for a moment studying the brick structure that had been built nearly a century ago. In the courtyard, three school buses were parked inside the chain link fence.

Lane and Harper walked past the buses and through the back door of the school.

"You really think this is the place?" Harper asked.

"Leo said the graffiti artist worked the neighbourhood and this is the nearest high school. Next door is an elementary. It fits the description." Lane turned left. They headed for the office. A glass wall separated it from the hallway.

In front of the office a group of students parted as the detectives approached. Lane opened the door. He and Harper walked inside the office. A woman of about fifty tipped her head to one side and said, "Yes?"

"We're detectives with the city police, and we'd like to talk with someone about Maddy Jones." Lane smiled at the secretary. *Nobody will mess with her,* he thought.

"That would be Murf." The secretary picked up the phone, punched four numbers, and said, "Couple of policemen here to see you about Maddy Jones." She nodded and hung up the phone. "On her way."

At the sound of footsteps on a hollow hallway floor, Lane looked to his left. The woman they were waiting for was little more than half Harper's height, had her brown eyes on them, and was steaming up the hall.

She stuck out her right hand and pushed back a wisp of unruly brown hair. "Anna McMurphy."

Harper pointed at Lane, "Detective Lane." Then at himself, "Detective Harper."

McMurphy cocked her head to the right. "My office is this way." She led the way. Their footsteps thumped along the carpeted hallway. She shut the door behind them and sat at the round table in her office. Lane and Harper sat across from her.

"I'm not sure why you're here. I haven't called the police yet." McMurphy looked at the ceiling when she realized her mistake.

"Yet?" Harper asked.

McMurphy rolled her eyes. "I wasn't sure if I should call

the police yet is what I was thinking, and what I wish I hadn't said."

Lane leaned forward. "Maybe this will help." He pulled out a series of photographs from a manila envelope. "These messages have been found on neighbourhood dumpsters. The last one warns that something is about to happen, and we think Madeline Jones may have the answer to what this is. You understand that all of what I've told you is confidential?"

McMurphy nodded. "And what I thought you were here for appears to be unrelated."

"At this point in the investigation, we would appreciate any information about Maddy. It may help us to better understand her in relation to this case," Lane said.

"Is this also a murder investigation?" McMurphy asked.

"That's correct." Lane nodded. *She's very quick*, Lane thought.

"I don't see how what happened today will help you."

Lane opened his mouth.

McMurphy silently worked through her dilemma.

Lane closed his mouth.

McMurphy took a breath. "I'm not sure where to begin."

Lane looked at his watch. "We've got time."

McMurphy looked out the window. "Madeline has been a student here for six years. She started in grade seven. Very bright, very quiet, very pretty. When she was in grade eight, there were rumours circulating that pictures of her could be found on certain sites on the Internet."

"What kinds of sites?" Harper asked.

"Porn." McMurphy frowned at Harper.

Lane shook his head. *I can see why she thought her information was unrelated.*

"Two days ago, I'd been unable to verify the rumour. Then I got a call from downtown. The school board monitors some web sites. One of the users from our school had logged onto a porn site. You have to understand; I've been trying to catch this person for three years. He would steal another person's password and log on. Several times, we've had to investigate young teachers who appeared to have logged onto porn sites and who denied having done so. A pattern emerged. It led me to a particular individual. For a long time it was like chasing smoke. This time, I walked into his office and caught him while he was logged on."

"A teacher?" Harper asked.

"Guidance counselor, actually." McMurphy looked at the door to ensure it was closed. "Recently, he called Maddy into his office, and she stormed out calling him a pervert. The secretary relayed the story to me."

"So, can we talk with the guidance counselor?" Harper asked.

"You can, but he's not here. He's at home. You'll need to talk with him and his lawyer."

"What about Madeline?" Lane asked.

"She's been away since I talked with her yesterday. She walked out of our meeting. I got the impression she was getting ready to tell me something important, but she got scared and left."

"What time was that?" Lane asked.

"About one o'clock."

About forty-five minutes before we saw her, Lane thought.

Could we see the counselor's office?" Lane asked.

"Sure." McMurphy led them out of the main office, into the hallway, and to the guidance office. She smiled at the secretary, who looked up at the detectives and smiled.

"Could we get into his office, please?" McMurphy asked.

"You bet." The secretary stood up, grabbed a set of keys from her desk drawer, and opened an office door. "Nobody's been in or out since he left yesterday."

Lane and Harper stepped inside. McMurphy followed

them and closed the door. Lane looked at the photographs. "Is this him?" Lane pointed at one photo.

"Yes." McMurphy nodded.

Herrence's pictures hung on three of the four walls; the remaining wall was windows.

"Over there." Harper pointed at a picture of Herrence with three other men.

Lane studied the photo of Smoke, Herrence, and Jones. "Fascinating."

"Who?" McMurphy asked.

"It's a group of men who like to drink scotch together." Harper looked around the office.

"We need to have someone go through this computer," Lane said.

"I see," McMurphy said.

"She has a little sister who's in elementary school?" Harper asked.

"Right next door," McMurphy said.

Five minutes after McMurphy walked them next door, they were sitting in the principal's office at the elementary school.

"Deborah Davies." She kept her hands behind her back and ushered the detectives into her office. Then she stood behind her desk and motioned for them to sit in the chairs facing her.

"We came to inquire about Madeline Jones' sister. We believe the younger child's name is Andrea," Harper said.

"Lovely child." Davies sat down, leaned over, and looked into the bush outside her window. She used her right hand to rearrange the pashmina scarf on her shoulders.

"Could we speak with her?" Lane asked.

The principal turned her head and pressed her cheek against the window. "I'm afraid that's impossible."

"How's that?" Harper asked.

"Not here. Her father and sister picked her up after school yesterday. Dr. Jones — lovely man by the way — said they're heading off for a family holiday to Cuba." Davies frowned and looked at the detectives. "Perhaps you could assist me with another matter?"

"Oh?" Harper looked at Lane.

"A stakeout. You see, the students from the high school are in the habit of copulating in the bushes outside of my window. I would like them arrested!"

×

"No one here." Harper held his hands out. They met in the backyard of the Jones' family residence, between the garage and the house. It was an oasis with an apple tree, wild flowers, lilacs, fishpond, and potted plants. The outside of the house was all stuccoed, except for the front, which was finished in river stone. The pillars at the front were coated in copper. The windows were circles of various sizes. Through a window, Lane caught glimpses of exotic woods used to finish the interior, in particular the great room. The three-car garage was bigger than the wartime house across the alley.

"Can't see anybody inside or out. Mail's in the mailbox." Lane took a look around the yard. *They must hire a gardener.*

"No car in the garage." Harper leaned over the pond. "Even the fish appear to have left."

"It looks like we need to get a description out. I wonder where he's headed?" Lane asked.

"At least we may have a motive now." Harper took off his jacket and draped it over his arm.

"How's that?"

"If this is about child porn, and Jennifer Towers found out, it could be the motive for her murder."

"Or it could be something else altogether. We need to talk with McTavish," Lane said.

×

Maddy set the bags of new clothes on the bed. For a few hours today, it had felt as if the stepfather she remembered was back. The man she had worshipped as a child. Before. Her life was always before. Before the pictures. Before the lies. Before the threats. Before the nights when he opened her bedroom door.

"How come daddy bought us all new clothes? Why can't we go home?" Andrea jumped on the bed and sat down next to Maddy.

"He says we're going on a holiday, and we need new clothes." Maddy took new socks and underwear out of a bag. She peeled off tags and labels. *You know, it would be so easy to walk out that door,* she thought.

"How come he said our name is Brown? Our name is Jones," Andrea said.

Maddy handed her a pair of socks. "Here, put these in your drawer." *I'm beginning to wonder what our name really is. Jones? Brown? Smith?*

"Why?" Andrea threw the socks on the floor.

"Because I need some help, and you're old enough now." *If he does what he's planning to do to Andrea, she'll never be the same.*

"No! You can't make me!" Andrea crossed her arms.

Andrea has no idea what it's like, and it has to stay that way. I can't let that happen to her.

"I hate you!" Andrea's foot shot out and caught Maddy in the chest.

Maddy slapped her sister across the face.

For a moment, they both froze. Andrea, with her mouth open and a red mark on her face. Maddy, with her hand stinging and guilt crawling into her gut because of what could not be taken back.

×

They found McTavish around the back of a coffee shop on Nineteenth Street. He sat in a green plastic lawn chair at a green plastic table. His police motorcycle was parked nearby, and his helmet sat on the table.

"Got time for lunch?" Lane asked.

"Already ordered. How about you?" McTavish smiled as his coffee arrived, served in a bowl.

Harper and Lane ducked inside to order coffees and sandwiches from a young black-haired woman wearing a worn Hello Kitty T-shirt and a ready smile.

Outside, they sat down with McTavish, who asked, "How's your niece doing?"

"Better, I think." Lane looked at Harper. "As far as I know, she hasn't been out late at night working on her graffiti."

McTavish nodded and smiled. "You wanted to know about Dr. Paul Stephen?"

Harper said, "It looks like his partner, Dr. Jones, is into some nasty stuff. Jones may have skipped town."

"Nasty stuff?" McTavish turned his head to one side.

"Kiddie porn is one possibility. Murder is another." Lane waited for McTavish's reaction.

"Shit." McTavish put his coffee down. "If I'm right, Paul Stephen is the money behind a car-theft racket. Working alone or with his brother, Stephen takes a look at what vehicles are hot around here, has them stolen down east, then sells them in the city."

"How's it work?" Harper asked.

"They steal vehicles that are less than a year old and have low kilometres. They have the VINs changed, ship them out here, and price them to sell. They make a tidy profit on each vehicle, especially considering they pay nothing for the cars. By the time we've caught up with the vehicles, the curber has moved on, or the used-car dealership is out of business. It looks like one of Stephen's brothers handles the eastern end while another handles this end."

"And Dr. Stephen launders the money through Jones' practice," Lane said.

Their coffees arrived, along with McTavish's sandwich.

Harper and McTavish watched Lane enjoy his first sip of coffee.

"Man, you love that stuff," McTavish said.

"You have no idea," Harper said.

"Any idea how we can get a hold of the good Dr. Stephen?" Lane asked.

"He and his brother move farther west every time there's any hint of heat, so they both may be gone along with Dr. Jones or..." McTavish stopped to consider another possibility. "Stephen has a girlfriend. High end. High maintenance. Lives in a house in Mount Royal. If you hurry, you might catch him there."

"How come you haven't pulled him in yet?" Harper asked.

"He's always kept enough distance from the stolen car operation. We haven't been able to prove a link yet." McTavish took his sandwich in two hands and bit into it.

"Got an address on the girlfriend's house? We could bring him in and question him about the murder," Lane said.

McTavish put the sandwich down and pulled a notebook from his jacket pocket.

Harper said, "I can't find any record of Stephen ever graduating university with a degree in dentistry."

Lane smiled at his partner. "So, we can talk with him about his phony credentials too."

×

Lane shut off the engine and sat listening to the end of a rhythm-and-blues tune. He glanced at the front door of his house. *Just sit still for a minute*, he thought. *If you don't move, and breathe slowly, it doesn't hurt.* A noise attracted his attention. He looked at the front door of his house. The door swung open. Alexandra stepped out with her suitcase and overnight case, with Arthur in tow carrying two oversized bags.

Alexandra's face was white-red with anger. Arthur looked over his shoulder and came close to tripping down the stairs.

Lane thought about getting out; instead, he reached for the switch for the passenger window. The window hummed open. "Need a lift?"

Alexandra's eyes swung around to meet his.

Don't mess with her, he thought.

"What's that supposed to mean?" There was fire in Alexandra's voice.

Pour water on it, he thought. "Wherever you're going, I don't think Arthur will be able to carry those very far." Lane glanced in the direction of her luggage.

Arthur set the bags down and wiped sweat from his forehead.

Alexandra looked behind her, laughed and turned back to face Lane. "How do you put up with that niece of yours?"

"I saw her being born. Loved her ever since," Lane said.

Alexandra's mouth opened.

Arthur stepped back as if shielding himself from an imminent explosion.

Alexandra looked at Arthur, then turned to Lane. Tears rolled down her face.

Lane and Alexandra sat in the Jeep for ten minutes. Arthur brought out a box of Kleenex and went back inside.

"I told her she was lucky. At least she has a family. Then Christine told me to mind my own business, that I wasn't abandoned by my father and mother." It took a couple of minutes for Alexandra to continue. "Then I told her I've hardly seen my mother since she got remarried, and my father is always traveling. When we're together, he hardly talks to me anyway. I thought if I really did have a sister at least then..." A fit of crying interrupted the rest.

Christine stormed down the steps and opened the back door. "What's she telling you?"

Lane turned and froze her with a stare. "Stay."

"No." Christine stood outside the door with her arms crossed over her breasts.

Lane glared at her.

Christine got in.

Lane thought, *I've handled domestic disputes before. I can handle this.* "You're sisters. You had a fight. Sisters do that. So, are you going to finish this relationship with a fight? Or are you going to talk and with the understanding that you are more similar than different?"

"Talk." Christine opened the door.

"Good. That's what this family does," Lane said.

"This family?" Alexandra asked.

"Well, you're here aren't you?" Lane looked at her and then at Christine. "Are we going to sit down for dinner or not?"

After they put Alexandra's bags back in the guest room, ordered pizza, talked some more, and got Alexandra unpacked, the sisters fell asleep leaning against one another on the couch.

Matt came in the back door, looked at them, looked at his uncles and said, "Interesting evening?"

Lane and Arthur looked at one another. They nodded silently with the intense fatigue following the explosion of the sisters' now-spent emotions.

"It's eleven o'clock." Arthur said, waiting for an explanation for Matt's late arrival.

"Dress rehearsal," Matt said.

"I've got to be up at five." Lane yawned.

✕

Maddy pulled a chair over to one of the windows on the west side of their hotel room. The glass stretched from floor to ceiling. The top and outside edges were stained glass. She looked down at Ninth Avenue. Headlights shone down the street at infrequent intervals.

She leaned forward to look down. Someone walked across the street against the traffic light. The pedestrian was illuminated by the glare of a car's headlights. The pedestrian ran to the curb.

Maddy sat back down. She looked out over the lights and silhouettes of buildings. The lights of an aircraft flashed red in the sky.

Andrea talked in her sleep.

Maddy looked around.

Andrea stuck her thumb in her mouth.

On the phone, he said he had to be at the border at six o'clock Friday evening. He had to wait because of the schedule. It was the only way he could get safely into the States. Then he said two people were crossing. Only two of them. Which two did he mean?... You know, Maddy thought.

She looked down at the street. An idea blossomed and she smiled.

chapter 17

Lane dreamed of a phone just out of reach. When his fingers finally touched the plastic, and the phone flipped open, his fingers only found wrong numbers. Finally, he was able to dial, but no one answered.

He opened his eyes. Around the edges of the curtains, light illuminated the wall and the ceiling.

The phone rang.

He reached for it and groaned from the pain of bruises, sore joints, and damaged muscles left over from the accident. The phone fell to the floor. "Shit!" Lane sat up.

Lane found the phone on the floor with his right foot and picked it up. "Hello!"

"That you, Lane?"

"What is it?" Lane asked.

"You okay? Sounds like you just fell out of bed or something," Harper said.

"Lane? What happened?" Arthur asked.

"I've got it," Lane said.

Arthur tapped Lane on the back. "What happened?"

Their door opened and the light came on.

Lane squinted.

"What happened?" Christine asked. "Oh my God! Put some clothes on, Uncle Arthur!" She slammed the door.

"Lane?" Harper asked.

"Go ahead," Lane said.

"Looks like our friend the artist is still in town."

"And?" Lane asked.

"This time there's been a change in location. Wrote the

message in ten-foot letters down the middle of Stephen Avenue Mall."

"What's it say?" Lane asked.

"Jennifer's killer leaves Friday. The media's all over this one."

"No kidding." Lane sat up and groaned.

"I'll be there in ten." Harper hung up.

×

Lane watched the pedestrians walking on either side of the avenue. Stephen Avenue Mall was taped off to traffic. Some people stared at the red letters painted on the pavement. Others sipped their coffees and listened to music, oblivious to the warning.

TV crews were set up at either end of the barrier. One camera operator stood on top of a van in order to get all of the words in her frame.

Lane scratched the back of his head, sipped at his coffee, and thought, *Was that three or four hours of sleep?*

"It was around four this morning." Harper lifted the lid on his cup of coffee. "The patrol car spotted the paint, but not the painter."

"So, if Malcolm's right, the artist is staying around here somewhere because she works whatever neighbourhood she's in. That means," Lane turned around to look at the hotels within sight, "she's within walking distance. It appears we need to find her by noon on Friday, or sooner. And we need to get some officers checking each of these hotels."

"What about Mount Royal?" Harper asked.

"Want to go and take a look?"

×

"Get packed!" Joseph Jones, wearing his bathrobe, stood in the doorway to Andrea and Maddy's room.

Maddy was instantly awake. She gauged the distance to the bathroom, then, looked to see how close Andrea was in case she needed to grab her little sister and run.

"Why?" Andrea asked.

"Never mind!" Jones turned his back on them. "We're leaving in fifteen minutes!"

×

The two-storey house was made of brick. Its roof was tiled red. Each window was clad with white metal. The driveway was a semicircle of pebbled concrete. Two gold Mercedes were parked in it. The front yard, except for the fir trees, was concrete and interlocking brick. Other houses on the block displayed manicured lawns, tulips, and trees.

"Boy, this house stands out." Harper parked behind a BMW. He could see the front door through the windshield of the BMW and Lane had a good view between a pair of lilac bushes.

In a few days the lilac blossoms will be out, Lane thought.

"That's one maintenance-free property," Harper said.

Lane took another look at the neighbour's place. Sprinklers popped out from under the trees, sending a fine mist into the air. Sunshine created a series of rainbows.

"What haven't we thought of?" Harper asked.

"Sounds like we were too late getting to the hotel. A man and his two daughters checked out fifteen minutes after the media reported the message on Stephen Avenue. It looks like Jones has access to more than one identity because the description matches him but the name doesn't. And we haven't interviewed Herrence from Maddy's school." Lane took a small sip from his coffee. He winced when his arm ached and his shoulder complained. *Make the coffee last; we could be here a long time.*

"I don't understand why Jones is hanging around town.

He knows we're looking for him, but he's still here. Doesn't make sense."

"It doesn't make sense. None of this makes sense. One phony dentist is into selling stolen cars, and the other looks like he's into kiddie porn. All they have to do is stick to the practice, and they'd make plenty of money." Lane looked at the house and thought for a moment. *We're wrong; it's beginning to make sense.* "So, what's the connection?"

"We have to look at this from another angle." Harper flipped down the visor and looked at his reflection. "Jones has disappeared with the two girls. The porn shots of Maddy were taken when she was about the same age as the youngest is now."

"That might explain the Maddy's graffiti warnings. The assistant principal at the school heard rumours about the pictures, and Madeline had an argument with her guidance counselor. She might be trying to protect the little sister. But why not just come to us?" Lane watched as the front door of Stephen's girlfriend's house opened. A slender woman wearing a red blouse and blue shorts stepped through the doorway and made her way down the stairs with two suitcases. She opened the trunk, dropped the bags in, and repeated the ritual three more times.

"She matches the picture on her license. Her name's Stephanie," Harper said.

Lane looked at the picture.

Stephanie closed the trunk, climbed into the car, and started it up.

"Wanna see if she takes us to her boyfriend?" Harper asked.

Lane nodded.

They waited until she turned the corner at the end of the street before following her. Harper managed to keep Stephanie in sight when she turned onto Fourteenth Street and travelled north down the hill.

Lane kept his eyes on her Mercedes. Harper worked at keeping at least one other car between them without losing her at a light.

After crossing the river, she turned west on Memorial then north west on Crowchild.

"If we're lucky, she'll lead us right to Paul Stephen." Harper stopped two cars behind her at a light.

"Think she's headed to his office?" Harper asked.

"I don't know," Lane said.

They followed her for ten minutes until she turned right, took an overpass, and turned into the parking lot of an inn next to Crowchild Trail.

Harper eased into the lot.

Stephanie stopped her car at the front doors of the inn.

"Let me out here." Lane opened the door, waited for Harper to stop, and stepped out. Lane eased the door closed. His back ached. He put his right fist on his hip while he walked up to the front doors.

Harper drove alongside Stephanie's Mercedes.

Lane saw her look to her right and smile.

Paul Stephen stepped out the front door, carrying a briefcase. His face and head were clean-shaven. His clothes were casual.

"Dr. Stephen?" Lane said to the suspect while nodding at Harper, who was watching his partner in the Chevy's side mirror.

Paul Stephen looked at Lane and then at Stephanie.

Harper accelerated and cut in front of the Mercedes.

Stephanie's car lurched forward. Glass smashed, plastic cracked, and tires squealed. Harper's car was broadsided.

Stephen turned to run. Lane grabbed his wrist. Stephen tried to pull away.

Lane caught a whiff of Stephen's aftershave and thought, *You'd think he'd know a subtle scent is better, much better.* He twisted Stephen's wrist and pulled the so-called doctor toward a pillar supporting the inn's roof. Adrenaline fueled Lane as he pulled out his handcuffs, snapped them over Stephen's right wrist, grabbed his left wrist, and locked the other bracelet so that Stephen found himself hugging the pillar.

Lane looked to his left. The Mercedes' rear tires were smoking as they crushed Harper's Chev up against the concrete of a light pole.

The smell of burning rubber caught at the back of Lane's throat as he walked to the passenger door of the Mercedes. Its tires howled.

Lane tried the door. Locked.

He leaned down and looked inside. Stephanie stared back at him, then looked away.

Lane pulled his Glock out of its holster, checked to see that the safety was on, and smashed the butt against the rear window. After the second blow, the safety glass shattered into pebble-sized bits that cascaded into the car.

He reached in and opened the lock for the driver's door. The screaming tires boiled smoke into the air. A cocoon of white surrounded them. He opened the door and leaned inside.

Lane looked at his Glock. He put his forefinger outside the trigger guard and pointed the weapon at Stephanie's nose. She lifted her hands away from the wheel. With his free hand, Lane shifted the car into neutral. The engine raced.

Lane kept his eyes on Stephanie.

Her eyes were on the gun.

He reached over and turned the key off.

Seconds later, in the silence, Stephanie said, "Stupid cop. You've got nothing on us."

"Two minutes ago that would have been exactly correct. Put your hands on top of the steering wheel." Lane kept his eyes on her. "Harper? You okay?" he called.

There was no answer. *I promised Erinn I'd look out for you*, Lane thought.

×

"How come we changed our name again?" Andrea asked.

Maddy handed her sister a pair of socks from the dresser. She smiled and hated the fact that Andrea put the socks away without argument. Andrea had become very accommodating since Maddy had slapped her.

The traffic noise from Macleod Trail snuck into their room through an invisible gap around the edge of the window. This time, they had an adjoining room with Jones. The door stayed open between the two rooms.

He stood there, in the doorway, his bathrobe open. "How are my girls enjoying their new room?"

Maddy looked out the window. *He's getting ready. Working his way up to it, just like he did with me.*

"Put some clothes on," Andrea said to her father.

"Yes, baby." Jones turned and walked back into his room. "Your wish is my demand."

"Daddy's weird." Andrea dropped the socks into her drawer and shut it.

×

"I want to know how Jennifer Towers died." Lane sat across the table from Paul Stephen. The room was a monochromatic, institutional yellow.

Next to Stephen sat his lawyer, Treneman, who actually wore a blue pinstriped suit and carried a black alligator-skin briefcase.

Cliché, Lane thought. *The suit probably means this lawyer is conventional. I'll give him what he expects for the first few minutes.* "I want to know how Jennifer Towers died."

"As we've already indicated, Dr. Paul has no knowledge of what happened to Ms. Towers," Mr. Treneman said.

Now throw in a bit of incriminating evidence, Lane thought. "In his luggage we found three separate passports with three different identities. All had Paul Stephen's picture on them." Lane watched the lawyer's eyes, and then watched Stephen.

Mr. Treneman glanced at his client, then focused on Lane.

Stephen shrugged. "We don't know where those came from."

"How did Jennifer Towers die?" Lane watched the lawyer frown.

"We've already answered that question." Treneman looked at his watch.

"Here's another detail." Lane looked at Treneman. "The good doctor here is not a doctor."

There was a knock at the door. Lane stood up and opened it.

Harper motioned for Lane to come out into the hall and shut the door.

"Stephanie's ready to deal. Her lawyer's ready to deal. Seems she had no idea that what she tried to do to a police officer could mean jail time. She'll tell what she knows in exchange for no jail time." Harper smiled.

"House arrest?" Lane asked.

"In that mansion of hers?"

"That's right."

"I'll check." Harper began to walk away. "Aren't you coming with me?"

"I just put a gun up her nose. It's not likely she'll want me there."

Harper turned and smiled. "That's exactly why I want you in on this."

Lane opened the door. "Wait, please," Lane said to Stephen and his lawyer. He followed Harper down the hall to Stephanie's interview room. Lane stood with his back to the door while Harper sat down.

Stephanie looked at Lane and snarled. "What's he doing here?"

"I asked him to be here," Harper said. "Now, tell us what you know in exchange for a recommendation for house arrest instead of jail time."

"House arrest?" Stephanie stood up.

Her lawyer looked at her.

Where do these guys come from? This lawyer looks the same as the other one, Lane thought.

Harper stood and turned to leave. Lane opened the door. Harper stepped outside. Lane followed, letting the door close behind him. "You see, you didn't want me in there."

Harper grinned. "It's been drama from start to finish. This is perfect. Just wait with me for a minute or two. Besides, the phony doctor may have a vivid imagination. He'll be thinking about what Stephanie is telling us. I get the distinct impression she's enjoying her own performance."

"So are you," Lane said.

"You betcha. She had her Mercedes jammin' me up against a light pole. I don't have much sympathy for her. Had a hell of a time getting out of there. We'll give her the chance to perform enough drama to get both of them locked up."

Someone knocked on the inside of the door. Harper opened it. The lawyer said, "Stephanie wants to talk."

Lane listened for ten minutes and left.

When he opened the door to the interview room, the former Dr. Stephen was the first to look up.

"Stephanie agreed to talk," Lane said.

"I never should have told her." Paul Stephen's scalp was sprinkled with sweat.

Lane waited.

"He gave her nitrous oxide to put her out. She was going to blow the whistle on him." Stephen's right knee began to bounce up and down.

"He?" Lane thought, *Draw him out slowly, carefully.*

"Dr. Jones. Jennifer caught him taking pictures of a kid." Stephen rubbed the top of his head.

"Kid?" Lane asked.

"A patient. Little girl. He used nitrous on her, undressed the kid, and started posing her, taking pictures. It was his thing, you know. Not mine." Stephen looked at his lawyer, who nodded.

"What's your thing?" Lane asked.

Stephen looked at his lawyer. "What kind of deal do I get?"

"That depends." Lane leaned forward.

"On what?" Stephen asked.

"Whether or not we're able to find Jones, Madeline, and Andrea in time." Lane placed his palms down flat on the table.

Stephen took a long breath and let it out slowly. "My part of the deal was moving the money through the practice."

"Where'd the money come from?"

"We put in orders for stolen cars from Toronto and Montreal, shipped them out here, and sold them. The profits were laundered through the dental practice. We had a few patients but rumours were starting to circulate about Joe's habits. It was time to move on." Stephen leaned back in his chair. "Joe found out through his connections that you guys were getting close."

"Connections?" Lane asked.

"He belonged to some scotch drinkers' club. Lots of important people who scratch each other's backs. He heard from the club that some cop was getting close to uncovering my side of the business."

"What was Jones' reaction?" Lane asked.

Stephen smiled. "He had a plan. Joe was confident he had enough money put away that he could move to the States and live somewhere warm."

"How did Jennifer die?" Lane asked again.

"As I said, she caught Joe in the act. She was threatening to talk. Joe grabbed her and put her out with nitrous oxide. He gave her too much."

Lane waited.

"Joe knew about Jennifer's boyfriend and figured if he kept on like nothing happened the boyfriend would take the fall."

"Who helped dispose of Jennifer's body?" Lane asked.

"Joe went shopping and bought a bunch of plastic wrap. He cleaned her up and conned me into helping him dump the body in some dumpster."

Lane thought, *Say this casually.* "How can I find Joseph Jones?"

Stephen closed his mouth. He looked at his lawyer.

Treneman shrugged as if to say, "You've told him everything else."

"I suspect you both went to the same person to get your false IDs. If I'm going to track him, then I need a way to contact the person who made the passports." *Now we'll see just how smart you are*, Lane thought.

"No way." Stephen tried to smile and failed. "I mean Joe is one thing. These people made it pretty clear about what'll happen to me if they're exposed."

Lane's rage went white hot. As it consumed him, one part of his mind thought, *Keep thinking!* "You think I care about you?" *Hold onto it, control it. Use it! Let him feel the rage in your voice.* "Right now, all I care about is Maddy and Andrea! Are we clear on that?"

Stephen shuddered.

"It's all been civilized up to this point." Lane had a vision of a toddler in a garbage bag. A little girl's hair. Her dead eyes. The stink of decay resurrected the memory in every detail. Then he saw the running shoes of another toddler's body. "Not any more! This is about two kids! Joe's into porn, and you've just confirmed he's a killer. Prison's a nasty place for guys like him. He's on the run with a lot to lose. I need a name and number now!"

Stephen gave him the number.

Lane wrote it down. "Name?"

"Sammy." The doctor-impersonator seemed to be shrinking in his chair. "Will you tell Sammy I told you?"

"Not unless I have to." Lane left the room.

×

"You're shaking," Harper took a sip from a bottle of water.

Lane did the same.

"Too much caffeine?"

"Too many memories." Lane looked through the bottle of water, trying to see things more clearly. "I'm forgetting something. Something important."

"We've got an appointment with Sammy. That's important."

Lane pointed with his bottle of water, "One of the scotch drinkers tipped Jones off that we were getting close to Stephen's car-theft operation."

Harper stared at him. "Smoke?"

Lane shrugged, then checked his reflection in the window of the shopping mall music store. Jeans and a red golf shirt. No Glock. No ID. Just jeans and a red golf shirt. That's what Sammy asked for when she said, "Just stand outside the bookstore in Market Mall, and I'll come up to you."

Harper looked at his watch. "I'll hang back."

Lane walked north. He took a sip of water, inhaled, and held it. *Relax. If you're nervous, Sammy won't come near you.*

A man in an electric wheelchair with an orange flag bobbing along behind weaved in and around pedestrians. His hand in a driving glove worked the joystick. The man whirred past Lane.

The smell of urine and sawdust from the pet store seeped out into the mall.

Lane arrived at the bookstore, which displayed its best-sellers out front. A clerk chatted with a customer.

Lane looked out into the mall. The supermarket was close by. That, and a department store. He counted five escape routes. *Sammy chose well,* he thought.

"Five thousand up front."

Lane looked to his left. A woman in a tank top stood next to him. She looked to be fifty and was pushing a baby stroller. "Sammy?" Lane asked.

"Got a problem with that?" Sammy looked into the stroller.

Lane couldn't see a child. Just blankets and what might or might not be the top of an infant's head.

"I'm here for names. Nothing else. A man is on the run with two girls who are in danger. I want their names." Lane watched as the woman glanced around her, looking for the quickest way out.

"I'm a police detective, and I'm not alone. Tell me what I need to know and you walk out of here."

The woman's eyes widened. "I'm not alone either."

Lane looked around him. A man taller than Lane and sixty pounds heavier seemed to be taking an intense interest in their conversation. "Good. Give me what I need, you help two kids who need help, and you walk away." Lane thought, *Now it's up to you, Sammy.*

Sammy shook her head. "Who's the guy?"

"Dentist. Original name is Jones. Wears a goatee. My height. Vacant look on his face. Has two daughters."

Sammy took one second to think. "Brown, Fowler, and Ramsay. You're right about him. Those girls are in danger."

She turned and walked away.

×

"Mr. Richard Herrence, you were Madeline Jones' counselor?" Lane and Harper sat across from Herrence and his lawyer. She had moved her chair as far away from her client as the room would allow.

Herrence nodded in the affirmative. "Yes." He looked at his lawyer as if asking for her approval. She watched the detectives through black-rimmed designer glasses with rectangular lenses.

Lane thought, *She finds her client to be revolting. We might be able to get a bit more information if we're not too obvious.* "Madeline has disappeared."

Herrence smiled with ersatz concern, "That's very unfortunate. She's a very troubled young woman."

"We'd like to find her and her sister as soon as possible. Any assistance you can offer us would be appreciated." Lane leaned forward, watching Herrence's reactions.

The counselor thought about the question for more than a minute. He rubbed his chin as he considered the problem, just as a professional should.

Lane glanced at the lawyer. She appeared to be using her tongue to work a piece of food out from between her front teeth.

Herrence asked, "How would it benefit me if I assisted you?"

The lawyer gave Herrence a look of disgust, but she said, "You really don't want to ask that question."

Good, she's warning Herrence only after he makes a mistake. Lane looked at Herrence. "That depends on the accuracy of the information."

Herrence looked at his lawyer, then said, "I don't see how I can help you."

"You knew Dr. Jones," Harper said.

"I never met the man," Herrence said.

Lane took a breath to keep his voice as calm and even as possible. "There is a picture of you and the doctor in your office."

Herrence looked to the left at the corner of the room above Lane's head.

"You and Dr. Jones drank scotch together, usually once a month. Did he convince you to keep an eye on his daughter in case she began to talk? You know, about the pictures he took of her and downloaded on the Internet porn site?" Lane asked.

Lane saw the sweat breaking out at Herrence's hairline. *I've already got an answer.* "Just how well did you know Dr. Jones? The evidence supports the conclusion that you and Dr. Jones were partners in the sexual exploitation of children." Lane made it sound like he was about to order an aperitif.

Herrence shook his head.

The lawyer watched her client and waited in silence.

"Dr. Joseph Jones said he wanted me to keep an eye on her. He said Madeline was his stepdaughter, and he told me where to find the pictures on the net. After that, I had to protect him to protect myself," Herrence said.

"Again, you really don't want to say that," the lawyer said.

You've confirmed more than you think Mr. Herrence, Lane thought.

Herrence closed his mouth before placing his hand over it.

×

Maddy looked across the table at her stepfather and sister. He'd insisted that Andrea wear a white dress, white socks, and white shoes. There was even a white ribbon in her hair.

Maddy wore a black blouse and pants, black eyeshadow, and black nail polish. She looked at her water glass. It was sweating tears.

"I've ordered all our favourite foods," her stepfather said.

"What's our name again? Or should I say, what is it to-day?" Maddy asked.

Dr. Jones smiled a knowing smile. He looked at Maddy. "No need to deny it. You both understand. This is something special between the three of us."

Maddy's attention shifted to her sister.

Andrea moved a centimetre away from him. He put his arm around her shoulder to pull her closer. Andrea sat back and frowned at her sister.

The waiter arrived with a tray and three plates. "Steak and lobster?"

Dr. Jones pointed at the empty space in front of him.

"Yes, sir." The waiter put the plate in front of Jones.

"Chicken Caesar salad?"

Jones pointed at Andrea and smiled.

"Then you must be the Greek salad?" The waiter set the plate in front of Maddy.

She thought, *I can't eat this. All I want to do is sleep, but I can't.*

"Here's your cutlery." The waiter handed Jones a steak knife and a fork, then said, "Will that be all?"

Jones nodded. He handed Andrea her knife and fork. "There you go, my darling."

Maddy felt a rush of memory that brought bile to the back of her throat. She swallowed and focused on her stepfather's steak knife.

"Here, let me do that for you." Jones leaned his chin on Andrea's head and placed the napkin in her lap.

Maddy saw the back of her stepfather's hand brush across Andrea's breast.

Jones reached for his napkin. "Do the same for me?" he said to Andrea.

Andrea looked at Maddy. There was confusion and fear in Andrea's eyes.

Maddy reached for the steak knife.

Jones continued to smile at Andrea, waiting for the correct response from her.

Andrea's mouth began to form a question.

Jones put his right hand on the table.

Maddy took the knife. In one movement, she lifted the knife and slammed the blade through his hand and into the table. Maddy released the handle.

Jones' looked at his hand. It was pinned to the table by the blade.

Maddy saw the puzzlement in his eyes when he focused on her. He took the knife and pulled it out.

Andrea's eyes went wide with shock. A nameless sound started somewhere at the back of her throat.

Maddy thought, *I made a sound exactly like that when I was your age.*

Jones focused on wrapping the napkin around his hand.

The maître d' arrived in black, white, and faux concern. "Is there a problem?"

"I seem to have cut myself." Jones smiled at the man.

The maître d' smiled. "Might I suggest you get the wound attended to right away? And if you do, we won't charge for the meal." He looked at Maddy. His smile died.

Andrea began to cry. She looked away from her sister.

I was trying to protect you, Maddy thought.

✕

"Arthur phoned. He left a message." Harper handed Lane a cup of coffee.

Lane took the coffee and thought, *Matt's play. It's opening night!* "What time is it?"

"Six-thirty," Harper said.

"But…" Lane was torn between finding Madeline and Andrea and being at opening night.

"There's nothing you can do here. We're tracking Jones down with the identities Sammy gave you. You need a change of pace anyway. Get your mind off the case." Harper pointed his index finger and his coffee cup at Lane.

"We need all the bodies we can get. If we don't find them tonight or tomorrow, we won't get another chance!" Lane felt caught between two choices. Tomorrow wasn't an option for either one.

"Look at me," Harper pointed a finger at his chest.

Lane shook his head.

Harper waited. "You're no good right now. Do us all a favour, and get away for an hour or two. This is how you work best. You get your mind away, even for a few minutes, then the answers start to come to you."

He's got a point.

"You want an escort?" Harper asked.

If I don't make it on time, Arthur's going to kill me. "If I leave right now, I should make it."

"Well?" The look on Harper's face said the rest.

Lane was on the road within four minutes.

✕

Maddy looked out the window of their new hotel room. Her stepfather was in the adjoining room disinfecting the wound, patching up his hand, and taking painkillers. He'd insisted on stopping at a large drugstore in between switching hotels. *He's always moving toward the south end of the city,* she thought.

One more night. I need to stay awake for one more night. Below her, the traffic moved in intermittent waves.

Andrea handed her an open bottle of water. "For you."

Maddy hugged her sister and took a sip. *Cold, delicious, and sweet.*

×

Lane walked two blocks from where he was forced to park. Someone in a ladybug costume juggled practice knives near the access to the school parking lot.

"Fergus," Lane said to the ladybug as he passed.

"Mr. Lane," the ladybug said.

"Thanks for helping Matt out."

The ladybug curtsied and juggled. "My pleasure."

Lane eased his way up the stairs and through the doorway, where signs printed on coloured paper led him along hallways and up stairs until he found the theatre.

A young woman looked up from a table just outside the door. "Are you Lane?"

He smiled.

"Hurry!" She stood, opened the door, and he stepped into darkness.

"This is our production of *The Birthday of the Infanta* based on an Oscar Wilde short story." The woman in the spotlight had long blonde hair and a voice twice as big as she was. "We ask that you respect the actors; they've put a great deal of preparation into this piece."

Lane's eyes were adjusting to the darkness. A seat along the back wall was available. He sat down.

After ten minutes of listening to a king, queen, and self-indulgent princess, he glanced at his watch. *Am I in the right theatre?* he thought, *Where's Matt?*

He looked into the crowd. Here and there luminous watch dials and cell phones appeared as members of the audience checked the time. Lane looked at the ten foot high windows along the east wall. *It does feel like a castle in here,* he thought. A general mood of restlessness settled over the audience.

A figure half-walked, half-crawled up the stairs, past Lane and down the aisle. Soon, the audience in the aisle seats began to take notice. The actor was dressed in tan-coloured sack-cloth. He reached the stage. A spotlight illuminated him.

It's Matt!

Matt looked up at the princess. His face was a portrait of childlike innocence. With a deformed body and a perfect soul, Matt's character worshipped the princess. Lane felt himself being drawn into the performance. For the rest of the play, Lane could not take his eyes off of Matt. Around him, Lane sensed that others in the audience were also becoming a part of the imaginary reality created by Matt and the other actors. *How can a person become older, yet remain so innocent, so isolated?* Lane thought. *Madeline!* He watched as Matt's character died. Lane thought of other children he'd been too late to save. He shook his head in an attempt to clear the memories so he could concentrate on the play.

Arthur, Lane, Alex, and Christine waited for Matt after the performance. As he walked toward them, they saw the residue of makeup, and the exhaustion in his eyes. The performance had taken all of his energy.

Christine hugged him.

Arthur was next.

Lane found himself weeping.

Matt looked at him, "Uncle? What's the matter?"

I almost missed this, Lane thought. "You were amazing," he said.

Arthur drove the Jeep home. Lane followed. His mind spun with images of the play and the case. By the time they arrived home, he knew he needed to call Loraine.

chapter 18

"Who did you call last night?" Christine poured herself a cup of coffee and mixed in milk and brown sugar. She looked out the kitchen window. The sky was brightening in the west. A robin began to sing.

"Remember Loraine?" Lane turned toward his niece and winced. Every limb had its own bruise and every muscle had its own complaint.

Christine nodded. "She and Lisa just had the baby?"

"Yes. I had a question I needed to ask her about trauma and emotional development." Lane sat next to the phone and looked into his half-full coffee cup.

"I don't get it." She sat down across from him.

"When I was watching the play, it made me think about what trauma does to children, how it affects them later on. I needed an explanation for a young woman's behaviour. Loraine is trained as a psychologist, so she knows what happens to people who have been traumatized."

"Like me?" Christine seemed to be studying her cup.

"You, Matt, Arthur, the two girls we're searching for, me. Loraine says the child usually learns to deal with the trauma, but there are often scars. Apparently, emotional development can be retarded by the experience. I was looking for answers to inconsistencies in her behaviour."

"Mine too?" Christine asked. "Alexandra said that I act strange sometimes; it's like having a five-year-old's mind in my body."

"Something like that. But the young woman I'm thinking about appears to be attempting to protect her younger sister.

All she has to do is tell us what she knows, then we can help her and her sister. Instead, she tags dumpsters with messages about a murder and an upcoming crime."

"You've never been controlled by a twisted adult, then." Christine sipped her coffee.

Oh, yes I have. "You mean a twisted male adult?"

"Yes. Whitemore was sick. He played with my mind. Made me want to please him, feel worthy of him. I despised him at the same time. It messed me up. After a while, I had to believe in him, let him control me, or leave. My mother believed him. He had such power over her. If I hadn't left Paradise when I did…"

"You didn't exactly just leave," Lane said.

"How did you know?" Christine's eyes were suddenly wary.

"That you helped burn the house down? I've known that for some time."

"How? How did you know?" Christine asked.

"I know you." He pointed his coffee cup at her. "You fight back. You're not the kind of person who will just take it and take it."

"I thought if you found out, you'd kick me out. I mean your house had just burned down too. Why would you keep someone around who helped burn down a house?"

Lane saw the tears and the fear in his niece's eyes.

The sobs and words burst from her. "I helped her fill the cupboards and closets with kindling. She was frantic. If we were caught, then Whitemore would have us excommunicated or worse. Then her daughter would be shipped off to Utah to be married to some fifty-year-old man. We planned the fire for a specific night after a big celebration. At two in the morning we figured everyone would be asleep. The house we were in was a bit apart from all the others. Still, we made sure there was no one inside, and her daughter was asleep in the truck."

"I thought you walked away," Lane said.

"She drove. I walked. We decided we'd have a better chance if we went in different directions. There's a highway within two kilometres of Paradise, so I walked there. A retired couple in a motorhome picked me up and drove me to the city. They were heading back to the city because their daughter was sick and needed someone to take care of her kids." Christine looked down at her hands.

Lane reached over and touched them. "No one was hurt."

"Not that I know of."

"I did some checking. There were no injuries, no complaints filed. In fact, very few questions were asked." Lane felt one of her tears fall on the back of his hand.

"Nobody asks too many questions; even the people in the surrounding communities keep their mouths shut. Whitemore does business with all of them. Towns are afraid that they'll lose money if Whitemore shifts his business to someplace else. He's got them all under his thumb."

"Two women fought back." Lane kept his tone matter of fact.

"Yes."

"What do you do when you think the law can't protect you, and you think you're on your own?" Lane asked.

"I don't know." Christine looked up at him.

"Tag a few dumpsters?" Lane smiled.

By the time the call came, Christine was asleep on the couch. Her hair and skin were tinged with the reds and yellows of the morning sun.

Lane caught the phone right after the first ring, "Hello."

"It's me," Harper said. "I think we may have something. It's a hotel on the south side. I'll fill you in when I get to your place. Ten minutes, okay?"

"I'll be ready."

×

At 5:45 AM they were just ahead of the morning rush hour. With lights and siren going, Harper had them there in under twenty-five minutes. Lane saw that blue and white patrol cars had the entrances and exits covered. Harper pulled up to the front doors of the hotel and followed Lane inside.

"Third floor?" Harper asked the round-faced manager standing behind the counter.

"Here you go," he said and handed over a key. "Rooms three-twenty-six and three-twenty-eight. I need the key back when you're finished." He looked at his computer monitor, dismissing the detectives.

Lane and Harper took the stairs to the third floor, where they met two other officers. "Any signs of movement?" Lane asked.

The officers shook their heads.

"We need one of you to cover the elevators. How many at the other stairwell?" Lane asked.

"Two."

"We need one at the door to the adjoining room." Harper pointed further down the hall.

One officer met them halfway down the hall.

Lane inserted the key. He looked to his right to the officer at the next door.

Harper nodded at Lane.

Lane listened for any sound of a reaction from within. There was a gentle rumbling.

He stood to one side and eased the door open. It smelled of disinfectant.

What is that noise? he wondered.

He peeked around the corner and took a quick look inside. "City police!"

The noise continued.

Snoring! Lane pushed the door open and went inside.

Harper checked the bathroom after Lane passed the closed washroom door.

They checked the door connecting the next room to this one. It was locked.

Madeline Jones lay on her back on the bed. It looked to Lane like someone had thrown a blanket over her. Sweat stuck her black hair to one side of her face. One arm was outside of the blanket.

Harper pulled the blanket back. She wore a black shirt, slacks, and boots.

"Madeline?" Lane touched her shoulder.

She mumbled.

Lane tapped her shoulder, "Madeline?"

Madeline's eyes opened and closed again. "Andrea?" she asked.

She's slurring her words, and her pupils are dilated, Lane thought. He looked over his shoulder at Harper. "We need an ambulance. She's been drugged. Check next door. It's my bet Dr. Jones and Andrea are gone." Lane handed the key to Harper.

Lane spotted a glass on the dresser. He took it to the washroom. As he filled the glass, he looked around. No towels, no soap, no shampoo.

He found Madeline sitting on the edge of the bed, her arms propping her up on either side. She threw up on the carpet. The stench of vomit permeated the room. She gasped. "The bastard lied to me."

Lane put the water on the night table. Harper put a garbage can at her feet.

She lifted her head, looked at the water. "What is it?"

"Water from the tap."

Madeline took the glass and gulped it down, studying Lane all the while. "How did you find me?" She swallowed, looked at the garbage can, and vomited again.

Lane shrugged and sat down on the bed across from her. The mattress sagged. He felt his back aching from just below his belt to just above his collar.

"What time is it?" She raised her head, looking around the room.

"About seven o'clock."

"In the morning?"

"Yes," Lane said.

"Friday?" Madeline asked.

"That's right."

"No time. He's going across the border at six tonight. No time!" Madeline looked over Lane's shoulder at the door.

He saw Madeline's eyes widen with terror.

She tried to stand, then sat back down. "Andrea!" She put her head in her hands and began to weep. In between fits of sobbing, she bent over the garbage can and threw up several more times.

"I need your help." Lane worked at keeping his voice low, calm.

"You don't understand! You don't know what he's planning to do to *my sister*! Andrea!"

Lane heard the voice of a child in the pain behind each of her words. "If you and I can keep thinking, we have a better chance of finding her," he said.

Madeline looked at him. She used the back of her hand to wipe away vomit and mucous. "It's too late!"

"We don't know that." Lane crossed his legs. He heard others come into the room, but did not look around. Instead, he motioned with his hand that Harper should keep them back.

"I do!" Madeline said. "I know it's too late!"

Lane felt hope dying in him, but forced it out of his voice. He thought, *Change direction.* "You found Jennifer's body?"

She focused on him. "How do you know?"

"It had to be you. You painted the message on the dumpster."

She turned her head to one side to look at him. "Yes."

"How did you know where to look?" Lane felt an excitement he couldn't explain or communicate. *She's backing away from the panic.*

She shook her head. "You don't know anything."

"You're right. I don't know very much."

"He always follows a schedule, a routine. When he first opened up the dental office, he'd dump his trash there because he wouldn't pay for a cleaner. It was his routine. When he wanted to get rid of something, he'd use that dumpster. Once he gets something like that into his mind, it's like he can't think of any other way. When I heard Jennifer was missing, I went and took a look. I knew right then he'd killed her." She leaned forward.

"Are you going to be sick again?" Lane asked.

"I don't think so. You know, I tried not to fall asleep!"

"You were drugged." Lane kept his voice matter of fact, like he was ordering a cup of coffee.

Madeline looked back at him. "Andrea gave me a bottle of water last night."

"Who gave her the bottle?" Lane thought, *Keep her thinking, working this through to logical conclusions.*

"That asshole! He told me if I kept quiet about what he did to me, then he wouldn't do the same to Andrea."

"You mean the abuse, and the pictures on the internet?"

"You must have talked to my 'guidance counsellor'." Madeline made no attempt to hide the disgust in her voice.

Say this very carefully, he thought. "Actually, Herrence was arrested yesterday."

"You're lying."

Lane shook his head.

"Yes, my stepfather took those pictures. Have you seen them?"

Lane shook his head. "No."

"Sick fucks!"

"Who?" Lane asked.

"Herrence. My stepfather. Kids at school."

"So, you made a deal with your stepfather to protect your sister." *We're almost there,* Lane thought.

He heard a siren approaching. *We haven't much time.*

"He promised me if I didn't go to the police, he wouldn't hurt my sister."

"Then he hurt Jennifer Towers, and that changed everything."

"I had to let you know somehow. If the truck came and emptied the dumpster, then you might never know." Emotion crept back into her voice.

"Without your help, we wouldn't have got this close to you and Andrea."

"Really?"

There it is again, the voice of a child. "You said your stepfather follows a schedule. What's so important about six o'clock today?"

"I heard him talking on the phone. He has to cross the border just after six. It's a scheduling thing or a timetable thing. I can't remember which."

"Do you remember anything else?" Lane thought, *It's three hours to the border. He'll leave before three o'clock.*

"He said that two would be crossing." Madeline sagged. "I should have known."

Now is the time. "Let's make one thing clear!"

Her eyes were wary as she raised her head.

"This is not your fault. This is his doing. Not yours." Lane held her eyes with his. "What he did to you is wrong. What he's doing is wrong."

Harper said, "The paramedics are here."

"Why are they here?" Madeline said.

"You were drugged, remember? You need to be checked over." Lane regretted the words when he saw the way Madeline's eyes went wild.

She shook her head. The movement was exaggerated by fear. "They're not going to touch me! Nobody's gonna touch me!"

"Look, we need to cover our butts," Harper said. "We have regulations we're supposed to follow."

She pointed at Harper. "You've got your rules and regulations." Madeline pointed a finger at her chest. "I've got *my* rules and regulations." She pointed at the male paramedics. One sported a goatee and close-cropped hair. "Neither one of them is gonna touch me!"

"Would you speak with a female paramedic?" Lane asked.

Maddy thought for a minute. "How long will that take?"

Lane looked at his watch. "Thirty minutes."

"Forget it. I'm fine." Madeline stood up, then sat back down.

"What's the matter?" Lane asked.

"I feel dizzy."

"When did you eat last?" Lane thought, *She looks so damned pale.*

"Yesterday or the day before." Madeline looked at the empty glass.

"Do you want to get something to eat?" Harper asked.

Madeline frowned before throwing up in the garbage can yet again.

Lane insisted she have a shower and change of clothes. They waited in the adjoining room. A female officer waited outside of Madeline's bathroom door. She was out in less than ten minutes. Her face was free of makeup. She crossed through the doorway into the adjoining room.

Lane sat at the table. Maddy sat down across from him.

Harper put a can of ginger ale in front of her. She sipped it carefully.

Lane thought, *Make sure she has a clear path to the bathroom.* He cringed as he leaned over and bumped up against the wall. His shoulder was still on fire from where it had hit the parked car and the pavement.

Harper sat on the end of the bed.

Madeline turned to him. "You got hit by that truck."

Harper pointed at his partner. "He did. Where one bruise ends another one starts." Harper's stomach growled.

Madeline smirked.

"How about we order some coffee from room service?" Harper asked.

Madeline shrugged. "Okay."

Harper moved across to the phone, checked for the number, and dialed.

"How's the head?" Lane watched Madeline sip her pop.

"Still a bit dizzy." Madeline looked out the window.

"You're calmer now." Lane thought, *Stay away from questions. Just state the facts.*

Madeline looked directly at him.

Her eyes are clearer now, Lane thought.

She said, "I know where to find him. We used to drive to the States every summer. We'd always cross at the same place at a certain time. And we'd always leave on time. I told you, he's a creature of habit."

Harper put the phone down. "Are you going to tell us?"

Madeline nodded. "Are you going to take me along?"

"That's not gonna happen," Harper said.

"I have to be there. Andrea needs me there. She's my sister. I'm all she's got." Madeline lifted her ginger ale and looked at them as she drank.

"I don't understand your stepfather and what he's doing," Harper said.

"He used to tell me it was something special between him and me. You have to understand I was a kid, and I trusted him." She looked outside, seeing something way beyond the horizon. "Then a rumour started at school about me being on the Internet. After I saw the pictures, I didn't trust him anymore. I heard my parents fighting about it one night. Mom made him promise it would stop, that he'd never do the same to Andrea. It did stop, but Mom was never the same. She liked the lifestyle good ol' Jones gave us. Mom started to drink. Then she got prescription drugs from him. This isn't her first trip to detox, you know."

Lane looked at Harper, who said, "We can't take you with us."

"He won't hurt her today. He's distracted. He's very fastidious." Madeline set the pop down.

"Fastidious?" Harper asked.

"He thinks he's a connoisseur. Calls himself a foodie. He wants everything to be perfect so he can savour it; to him it's like food and cars. He wants it to be perfect with my sister." Madeline's eyes looked tired again; her voice was flat.

"Savour?" Harper asked.

"I saw it in the way he was treating Andrea last night. It was the way he treated me." Her eyes were vacant. "But I fixed him for a day or two."

She sounds like a child again, Lane thought.

"How?" Harper asked.

"Stabbed him through the hand with a steak knife. He'll still be bleeding and in pain. If he fucks Andrea now, it won't be perfect. He wants it to be perfect when he films it."

There was a knock at the door.

Harper got up and returned with a carafe of coffee and four cups. "That doesn't change the fact that you aren't coming with us. Besides the fact that it's dangerous, there are so many regulations against it…"

Madeline leaned forward and pointed at her chest. "I know the car. I know his license plate. I know where he'll be and when. Either you take me with you, or I leave now and do this on my own." She stood up.

Lane smiled. "And leave us to drink all of this coffee by ourselves?"

There was another knock at the door.

Harper opened it.

A female paramedic stood in the doorway with her carrying case.

"Come on in," Lane said. He and Harper waited in the next room as the paramedic examined Madeline.

After ten minutes, she joined them in the adjacent room while an officer sat with Madeline.

"Coffee?" Harper asked.

She nodded, pushed black hair back from her forehead, and accepted a cup from Harper. "I'm not a doctor, you understand. I can't make a diagnosis."

"I'm Lane and he's Harper." Lane reached to shake her hand.

"Elaine." She shook Lane's hand and then Harper's.

Give her a chance to think this over, Lane thought.

"I recommended that she go to the hospital. She refused," Elaine said between sips of coffee.

"I'm not surprised," Lane said.

Elaine looked at the detectives. "She told me she needs to find her sister. That her stepfather has the little girl?"

Lane nodded.

Harper said, "That's correct."

Elaine inhaled. "If I were a doctor, and you understand I'm not…"

"We understand," Harper said.

"If I were a doctor, I'd say Madeline's severely dehydrated and in need of bed rest. She needs to push the fluids and get some food in her stomach when it'll stay down. I'd also say I'd like to run some blood work to find out exactly what was used to drug her." Elaine looked at the door and moved toward it. "At least that's what I would say if I were a doctor."

×

"Detective Lane?"

Lane recognized the voice on his cell phone. "Chief Smoke." Lane nodded at Harper as they walked across the parking lot with Madeline between them.

"You are making progress on the Towers case." It was a statement of fact.

Who has been talking to Smoke? Lane thought. *Tell him only what he needs to know.* "That's correct. We are working on a tip and preparing to arrest a suspect."

"The suspect is?" Smoke asked.

"Dr. Joseph Jones." Lane walked around the Chev and leaned an elbow on its roof. *You know, Joseph Jones — your drinking buddy.*

Smoke was silent for a full thirty seconds.

Lane glanced at Harper, who was opening the back door for Maddy.

Smoke said, "I'm sorry to hear about your father."

To Lane there was the hint of a threat in Smoke's voice and something like gloating. Lane said, "Yes, sir."

"Any errors made in the investigation of this case will be attributed to you. I expect your report by the end of the day." Smoke said.

"Of course." Lane closed his phone. He got in the car and turned to Harper. "It's on my head, not yours."

×

They sat together in the Chev in the parking lot of the passport office next to Macleod Trail. Madeline glanced at the variety of unmarked police vehicles gathered around them. She heard Harper explain to the other officers what they were about to do.

Lane groaned as he turned to look over his shoulder at Madeline.

"I didn't mean for you to get hit by that truck. I'm sorry, you know." Madeline kept her eyes on the traffic whispering southbound along Macleod Trail.

Lane handed her a pair of binoculars. "What's the plate number?"

"Not yet." She adjusted the binoculars.

"What colour is the Mercedes?" Lane asked.

"Silver."

Lane picked up a two-way radio and passed on the information. His window hummed open. He breathed in the spring air.

"What are you going to do?" she asked.

"Get Andrea back safe. That's the first priority, then arrest Dr. Jones."

"What about me? Do I go to jail?"

There it is again, the voice of a child. "What for? You've done nothing wrong."

"It doesn't feel that way. It feels like it's my fault."

Lane looked at her. She glanced away from the binoculars for a moment. There were tears in her eyes.

"What happened was done to you. You were used, taken advantage of. You were betrayed." Lane watched her watching the traffic.

"You can say that, but it doesn't change the way I feel."

"What's on the license plate?" Lane asked.

Madeline looked through the binoculars. "Here he comes."

Lane spoke into his radio, "We're on!"

"The silver Mercedes. It's him." Madeline followed the car with the binoculars.

Lane asked, "Silver Mercedes four-door sedan?"

"Yep. I can't see *my sister.*"

Lane heard the tension in her voice. "Does she usually ride in the back seat?"

"Yes." She gave him the plate number.

Lane spoke into the radio, "Silver Mercedes four-door sedan. Watch for a child in the back seat."

The police vehicles left the parking lot and accelerated south on Macleod Trail.

Lane passed on the plate number and waited until the last vehicle, a blue pickup truck, left. He asked, "Buckled up?" Lane accelerated and followed the other vehicles.

Maddy nodded. She kept looking through the binoculars from the back seat.

"Will they hurt her?" Maddy asked as the police vehicles took up their positions in each of the three lanes.

Lane watched the vehicles, knowing that Harper was driving the Ford full-sized van in the left-hand lane. "Harper will do a visual to see where your sister is, then they'll set up and box Jones in so that it will be easy to extract her without him running."

"Won't he recognize Harper?" She had shifted the binoculars to focus on the van.

Lane glanced to his right. "He's wearing a ball cap, sunglasses, and a bright red jacket, and the side windows of the van are so heavily tinted that it's difficult to see inside."

Maddy looked at Lane for an instant. "I hope you're right." She turned her attention back to the Mercedes.

They watched from at least one hundred metres to the rear as Harper closed in on the Mercedes. He waited for the moment when the car in front of him signaled and eased into the left-hand turning lane. Harper moved up directly on the driver's side of the Mercedes, matched its speed for four or five seconds, then slowed until he was twenty metres back.

Lane and Maddy heard Harper's voice over the radio, "The child is in the back seat, driver's side. Looks like she's watching a movie. There's a handgun on the seat beside the driver."

Maddy nodded. "He got the gun a few years ago on one of his trips to the States."

Lane watched the pickup truck and van move forward.

The Mercedes pulled up alongside a city bus.

Lane watched the vehicles brake for a red light. The unmarked pickup truck pulled up behind the Mercedes. Harper, in the van, positioned himself next to Jones. Driver's side. Rear fender. The dentist's blind spot.

The light turned green.

Lane caught motion to the right. "Oh no."

A white semi pulling two trailers filled with gravel was moving east. The driver sounded his air horn in warning. The horn died.

Lane watched the heads of drivers ahead of him as they reacted to the wail of the horn.

The noses of accelerating vehicles dipped as they braked.

The silver Mercedes accelerated.

Lane heard the jake brake slowing the engine of the semi. The braking wheels of the truck were shuddering and bouncing on the pavement. The weight of the loaded trailers pushed the semi into the intersection. The rear tires smoked and screamed. The flat nose and chromed bumper of the truck plowed into the front door of the bus.

The bus skidded left and piled into the pickup driven by the police officer.

Lane saw the airbag explode in the driver's face.

The pickup skidded left, hitting the right rear bumper of Harper's van. The van spun to face the bus.

Harper was now visible through the van's windshield.

Lane saw the airbag deploy in Harper's vehicle when the

van and bus butted heads.

Vehicles behind the wreckage braked and skidded. The orderly lines of vehicles became a mass of metal and plastic scattered across the roadway.

Some crashed into the main wreckage of the bus and semi. Others remained unscathed in the midst of crumpled vehicles.

Lane stopped.

He reached for the radio to give the location of the accident on Macleod Trail. "We need ambulances, fire, and police. This is a multiple impact collision involving a city bus."

"He's getting away!" Maddy's hand slapped Lane's shoulder.

Lane looked in the mirror. Her eyes were wild with fear, and the shock of defeat.

Lane saw Harper step out of the van. He looked at Lane and pointed to the right lane. All of the wreckage had been pushed to the left side of the southbound lanes. The right lane remained partially open.

Lane shoulder-checked, accelerated, and cruised past the bus. He braked, turned sharply right, and turned left to move around the second trailer hitched to the jackknifed semi. He looked up at the rear bumper as he eased between it and the curb on his right side.

They squeezed through the gap without touching on either side.

Lane looked left. Harper was running alongside the semi. "I'll take care of this, you go!" He pointed south in the direction of the receding Mercedes.

Lane nodded. He checked left and right, saw he was clear, and pressed the accelerator. The engine responded.

"Keep your eyes on the Mercedes!" Lane looked in the mirror at Madeline. Her eyes met his before she lifted the binoculars and aimed them down the highway. "I'm going to keep well back. I need you to keep Jones and your sister in view."

Lane thought, *I don't think Jones saw us coming. That means he still thinks he's in the clear. He'll be at his weakest point when he thinks he's made it. Think ahead! Plan it out! That's what he does. He plans ahead! So stay one step ahead of him!* "Did Jones always go through the same border crossing when you went to the States?"

"Always. He always went the same way, and he always knew the customs guy at the booth." Maddy kept her eyes on the Mercedes. The distance between the two vehicles was gradually closing. "Can't remember his name, but they knew each other."

"Which border crossing?" Lane asked.

"Coutts."

Lane worked out the details in his mind. He looked at the clock on the dash and saw that fifteen minutes had passed since the crash. Lane reached for his phone and dialed. He waited for a few seconds. "Harper?"

"Lane? You still on him?" Harper asked.

"That's right. You okay? Any injuries?" Lane looked to his right. The mountains were there on the horizon. On his left, the prairies stretched all the way to Saskatchewan and beyond.

"Minor stuff so far. Couple of people on the bus got thrown around. One has a broken arm. It was lucky the semi hit the door of the bus. It could have been a lot worse. What about you?" Harper asked.

"I think we need to grab him when he reaches the border. That's when he'll be the most confident, and there will be a reduced risk to the child. Maddy says Jones knows a border guard. They always see the same one. That would explain the schedule, and the need to hang around waiting for a specific day and time. It also means we know when and where. So I need you there to coordinate with the RCMP. Everything will need to be ready for us at that end. And Harper?"

"What?" Harper's voice was barely audible.

"We want the border guard too. It looks like Herrence, Dr. Jones, and the guard are connected. We need to get them all. Got that?" Lane asked.

"I'm with you. Talk to you when I'm in the air." Harper's voice was gone.

"You're going to wait to get them at the *border*?" Maddy's tone of voice said she wasn't pleased with Lane's plan.

Lane glanced at Madeline. "Yes. I know you're thinking: things went wrong the first time, and they could go wrong again. But if we wait for the border, there is time to get set up and turn the odds in our favour. If we act now, at highway speed, it's dangerous for Andrea. Anything could happen. We have to outsmart Jones."

"It's not that hard. I've been doing it for years. He always has a plan and sometimes a backup. When both of his plans don't work out, he doesn't know what to do next." She kept her eyes on the road ahead. "When we get close, I'll get on the floor so he won't see me."

"Good idea." *Maddy's up to speed. And she's got to stay inside the car when we reach the border,* Lane thought.

"Now you're thinking about what you need to say to me so I'll do what I'm told. I can read your mind sometimes, too." Maddy didn't smile, but her tone of voice sounded a little less defeated.

"Can we agree that the first priority is to keep Andrea —and her sister— safe?" Lane asked as they passed a motorhome with a satellite dish. The RV was towing an Audi sports car.

"I agree, we get Andrea out." Maddy leaned back in her seat, her eyes still on the Mercedes.

Don't argue the finer points with Maddy. She heard you. Move on. "Aren't you feeling car sick from looking through the binoculars?"

"I don't get carsick." Madeline kept looking through the binoculars. "Sometimes I can see the top of Andrea's head, or her arms if she stretches."

"You're going to need to relax a bit every once in a while. We both need to be sharp in about two hours." Lane looked at the clock and wondered when Harper would call.

Half an hour further down the highway, Lane glanced in the rear-view mirror. A red minivan was approaching them from behind.

He looked at his speedometer. It registered 120 kilometres per hour.

In his rear view, Lane saw a pair of white socks on the dash on the passenger's side. He caught the silhouettes of two infant car seats in the back. The driver was talking to the passenger.

The van passed the Chev as if Lane were loping along. He watched the red van race away.

"There's another wonderful family. Two kids in the back. Parents racing down the highway. In a big rush to mess up their kids' lives." Maddy's tone was sarcastic.

Land watched the van pass two cars, then the Mercedes.

"Aren't you gonna tell me I'm wrong? Give me a talking-to because not all families are as screwed up as mine?" Maddy asked.

Lane shook his head. "You've got a point."

"You're kidding?" Maddy glanced away from the binoculars to get a glimpse of Lane's expression.

Lane glanced back at her, then watched the van and the Mercedes disappear over the crest of a hill. "Nope."

"We used to drive down into the States two or three times a year. My mom would go shopping. My stepfather would meet with his friends. Andrea and I would hang around the hotel. It was easy for me to keep an eye on her that way. Jones used to write the whole thing off as some kind of business trip. In reality, he was hookin' up with his porno buddies."

Maddy peered down into the valley as they descended. The Mercedes was climbing up the other side of the valley.

"How did you know about the porno buddies?" Lane asked.

"He started taking his laptop with him. A couple of times I checked what was on it while he slept. Kiddie porn."

"How long have you known?" Lane checked the time. *We'll be there sooner than you think. Keep sharp!*

Maddy's mouth moved as she chewed her lip. "Long time. Since Andrea was little. I've been watching out for her since she was born. She's really my stepsister, but we've always been really close. She's family."

I wonder how you'll handle it when you don't have to protect her from Jones anymore? Lane thought.

Twenty minutes later, Lane's phone rang. He flipped it open with his thumb. "Cam?"

Madeline glanced his way before focusing on keeping the Mercedes in her sights.

"Yes," Harper said. "We just landed and should be in place in fifteen minutes."

"We're about ninety minutes out. The Mercedes is still in sight. It appears the child is okay." Lane watched the Mercedes. It shimmered. Heat ran like silver over the top of the pavement.

"The plan is to go inside the main building at different times so we don't alert the border guards in the booths. We're all in street clothes. Local authorities from both sides of the border will be there to help with arrests. All transportation will be unmarked. No heavy weapons will be involved because of the child, and because that would draw attention to our arrival. The plan is to distract the driver and snatch the child." Harper paused. "Got it?"

Lane said, "I'll take up a position at the rear of the Mercedes and to one side."

"What about your passenger?" Harper asked.

"She'll be on the floor. Back seat. Passenger side." Lane looked in the mirror at Madeline. She looked back and nodded.

"Understood. Keep in contact." Harper hung up.

"We're agreed that you'll be on the floor before we get to the border?" Lane asked.

Maddy nodded. "Yes. And we're agreed that Andrea will get out safely?"

"That's our first priority," Lane said.

"I checked up on you, you know. You were involved in two other cases where parents killed their children." Maddy said.

"When did you do that?" Lane tried to keep his surprise hidden. *This one has survived by her wits. She's no fool.*

"After you chased me and got hit by the truck. I figure if you've seen two dead children, you won't want to see another."

"You're right about that." Lane kept his eyes on the road while haunting memories threatened to break his concentration.

"Andrea has a better chance with someone like you."

"And you," Lane said.

"What do you mean?"

"You need Andrea in your life and she needs you in hers." Lane kept his tone matter-of-fact.

Madeline nodded. "My back is sore."

"Take a break for a few minutes. After that, we have to be totally focused."

An hour later, they left the outskirts of Lethbridge and took the highway heading south to the border. The highway narrowed, and Lane saw that the Mercedes was decelerating.

"There's Andrea." Madeline's voice swelled with hope. "Oh no! She's climbing over the seat to sit beside him."

"Is she putting the seat belt on?" Lane asked.

Maddy nodded. "Yes."

Lane reached into his jacket pocket to check for the knife he'd brought just in case he needed to cut the seat belt to get Andrea out.

They coasted as they approached the US border. He flipped open his phone and dialed. "Harper?"

"Our spotter just reported the Mercedes," Harper said.

"We'll be next. Be advised that the child has moved into the front passenger seat."

Harper took a breath. "Understood."

That complicates things, Lane thought.

"What does it mean?" Madeline asked.

"Ask me in five minutes." Lane glanced over his shoulder to smile at Maddy. "When I tell you, release the seat belt and get on the floor."

He looked ahead, matching speed with the Mercedes, obeying the signs, easing into the next lane, pulling down the sunshade, and positioning his vehicle on the passenger side, in the Mercedes' blind spot. "Get on the floor." Lane listened for the release of the belt and the sound of Maddy's clothing sliding over the seat.

The Mercedes pulled into the left-hand lane.

A red minivan swept past Lane and braked to position itself behind the Mercedes. It was the same van that had passed Lane and Maddy on the highway.

Perfect, Lane thought as he took the left lane. The van obscured Jones' rear view.

Jones stopped in line behind a sedan. The roof of the border crossing provided shade.

Lane kept his head tucked close to the pillar on the left side of the windshield.

"How close are they?" Maddy asked.

Lane pretended to rub his nose. "Just one car length ahead."

Nearly five minutes passed before the Mercedes pulled up to the stop sign and waited for the next opening. Lane watched the border guard hand the passports back to the driver of the sedan in front of Jones.

The brake lights on the Mercedes blinked off.

The border guard waved Jones forward.

Lane watched as the driver of minivan pulled up to the stop sign.

Jones handed the border guard two passports.

Lane eased his Chev into park and readied his left hand to open the door. He checked for the knife in his left pocket.

The border guard smiled and talked with Jones.

A woman stepped from a side door to Lane's right and walked across the pavement. She pulled out her ID card while approaching the Mercedes from the passenger's side.

Jones' border guard ignored her. He glanced at the passports.

The woman made a right turn and walked alongside the driver's side of the Mercedes.

Lane saw a question forming on the guard's face as he turned to watch the woman.

A black suburban came the wrong way up the road and braked nose to nose with the Mercedes.

Lane opened his door and stepped out. "Stay here," he whispered.

With her left hand, the woman cuffed Jones' left wrist. She pulled on the cuffs until Jones' head and left shoulder were out of the window. Her sidearm was out and touching the back of his neck.

Lane ran forward and opened the passenger door of the Mercedes. He reached in with his left hand, keeping his eyes on Jones, who said, "What are you doing to me and my daughter?"

Lane shoved the transmission into park, pulled the key from the ignition, and stuffed it in his pocket. He looked to his left at Andrea's wide-open eyes. "Want to see Maddy?"

Andrea nodded.

Lane saw the fingers of Jones' bandaged right hand reaching between the seat and the console.

Jones eased his right hand up, revealing the butt of a handgun.

Lane thought, *Maddy's right. You really are stupid. You put Andrea's life at risk, and you abuse your stepdaughter.* He looked at Jones' eyes and saw a smile on the dentist's face.

Lane punched Jones on the elbow of his right arm.

Jones screamed.

Lane punched Jones' bandaged hand.

The weapon exploded.

The officer bent Jones' left elbow inside out against the doorpost. He screamed again.

Lane took Jones' gun, ejected the clip, disassembled the weapon, and threw the pieces into the back seat.

Lane snapped a handcuff on Jones' right wrist, then heaved the other end up and clipped it to the steering wheel.

Jones' looked directly at the detective. "I've got powerful friends who will ruin your career."

Lane smiled. "You've got friends who will run for cover when they find out what you've been up to."

Lane released Andrea's seat belt and took her hand. He helped her out of the car. He looked around. Plainclothes officers and uniformed border guards surrounded him with their pistols raised and aimed.

An American officer was cuffing the border guard, who

had dropped Jones' passports.

Another officer slid into the seat next to Jones.

Lane tossed him the handcuff keys, walked back to his Chev, and opened the back door.

Maddy looked up and saw her sister. "When I heard the gunshot, I..."

Andrea opened her arms.

Maddy sobbed and tried to pull herself up.

Andrea put her arms around her sister.

"I'm sorry," Andrea said.

"Are you okay?" Maddy asked.

Andrea nodded. "Daddy made me leave without you. He said we'd come back for you after you had your sleep."

"It's okay." Maddy sat up and hugged Andrea. "It's okay."

"Maddy, you're squishing me," Andrea said.

×

Lane glanced in the rear-view mirror. A pair of oncoming headlights illuminated Madeline. She slept with her head leaning against the door. Andrea was snuggled up next to her; the curve of one tucked into the hollow of the other.

Lane looked ahead at the red taillights of the semi trailer he was following north along the four-lane highway. He signaled left and pulled into the passing lane.

What's next? Lane accelerated and glanced at Harper, who snored as he leaned against the door on the passenger's side.

Lane concentrated as they passed the semi. Its tires howled as they moved alongside. Once he passed the semi, the lights of the truck lit up the inside of the car.

She's almost eighteen, Lane thought, *there might be a way. They're going to someone to make sure Maddy and Andrea stay together. And I know the right lawyer.*

"You okay?" Christine asked when Lane opened the front door.

"What are you doing up? It's two in the morning." Lane hugged her around the shoulders.

Christine turned her nose up. "A little stinky."

"Oh. Sorry." Lane backed away. "It's been a long day."

"The news said a little girl was rescued at the border. That her father was trying to escape. He was into kiddie porn?" Christine asked.

"And murder." Lane moved to the kitchen, opened the fridge, and picked out a bottle of beer.

"The woman in the dumpster?" Christine asked. "Chief Smoke was on the news talking about it."

"There was a group of us working together to catch the killer."

"So, who pulled the kid out of the car?" Matt stood at the top of the stairs, dressed in sweatpants and a T-shirt.

"What are you doing up?" Lane grabbed a glass, sat down, and poured the beer.

"We had our cast and crew party. I just got home." Matt sat down next to Christine. "Are you going to answer my question?" he asked.

"I pulled her out while another officer cuffed the driver. Harper orchestrated the whole operation." Lane sipped the beer.

"See, I told you," Matt said to Christine.

She smiled. "You need a shower, uncle."

chapter 19

"We have some news for you," Lane said as he and Harper stood on the front doorstep of the Towers' home.

"Come in." MaryAnne Towers was dressed in a pale blue housecoat. They followed her into the kitchen and sat down.

This case has been tough on all of us, but it hit her the hardest. Lane eased himself into a chair and watched Harper do the same.

"Want a cup of coffee?" MaryAnne combed her fingers through unruly hair. It looked as if she hadn't slept.

Lane got up. "I'll get it." He opened the cupboard above the coffee machine, grabbed two cups, and poured. He leaned across the table and topped up MaryAnne's coffee.

After handing Harper a cup, Lane sat down.

Harper asked, "We should talk with your husband, too."

MaryAnne stared at Harper. "Don moved out. He didn't like me visiting with James at the hospital. Thought I was wrong about the boy. We had an argument, and Don left." She looked at them, waiting.

"We believe we have the man who killed your daughter," Lane said.

MaryAnne went to sip her coffee, and put it back down on the table.

Harper sat up straighter and grimaced with pain. "It was Dr. Jones. Jennifer must have discovered what the doctor was doing to some of his patients, and he killed her for it."

MaryAnne chewed her lip. "Did she suffer?"

"We don't think so. We believe he used an overdose of nitrous oxide to kill her. She just never woke up." Lane readied himself when Jennifer's mother leaned forward.

"We have the testimony of one man implicating Dr. Jones. We also have evidence from the plastic wrap on Jennifer's body. DNA tests should connect Dr. Jones to the murder. We came to let you know that we caught the doctor at the border last night and he's in custody." Harper opened his hands on either side of his coffee cup.

MaryAnne shook her head. "So James had nothing to do with it?"

"James was telling the truth," Lane said.

MaryAnne got up. "He'll need to hear this. I'd better get to the hospital."

×

"I'm sorry. I should have realized." Lane talked on his cell from a coffee shop on Kensington only a few blocks from Andrea and Madeline's house on Oxford Street. He looked across the table at Harper, who was frowning.

"What's happened?" Harper sat up straighter, wincing from the after-effects of yesterday's collision.

"Can you call me back in five minutes?" Lane nodded and closed the phone.

"Madeline and Andrea are surrounded. Reporters. Porno dentist father, car-stealing partner, mother in rehab, and a murder. That's a week's worth of news," Lane said.

"At least." Harper put down his coffee cup and looked at his watch. "You said that Maddy and Andrea needed a lawyer."

Lane looked closely at Harper.

"Sometimes you talk to yourself." Harper lifted his cup and raised his eyebrows. "I was only dozing in the car last night. I heard."

"Why were you looking at your watch? Were you thinking it's time for lunch?" Lane thought, *We've been working together long enough that we just know what the other is thinking.*

"I was thinking about a particular restaurant," Harper said.

Lane thought, *Of course you were!*

"But first, what are you going to say to Madeline?"

The phone rang.

"Maddy?" Lane asked.

×

Lane pulled up across the street from the Jones' home. In front of the house, reporters lounged under the trees next to the sidewalk. When he crossed the street, the microphones appeared.

He made his way to the gate and turned to face the various media outlets.

One woman checked her lipstick in a compact mirror. A man brushed his hair while running his tongue across his teeth.

Lane looked over his left shoulder to see reporters appearing from behind the house. He walked through the line of cameras onto the street and waited for them to turn in his direction. *Now, when their backs are to the house,* Lane thought.

"What can you tell us about the crimes committed by Dr. Joseph Jones?" the female reporter asked.

"He has been arrested and will appear in court." Lane saw Harper's head appear around the back of the house and then disappear.

The reporter rolled her eyes as if to say, "We know that! Tell us something we don't know!"

The male reporter smiled at his competition's frustration. "Apparently, Dr. Jones is to be charged with the murder of Jennifer Towers, whose body was found within a block of this house."

Lane smiled back. "He is to be charged with murder, that's

correct." He watched Harper appear and wave at him from behind a Colorado blue spruce.

The female reporter shook her head. "Are you aware that Mrs. Jones, the doctor's wife, died of heart failure half an hour ago?"

Lane thought, *Oh no! Madeline and Andrea haven't heard yet.* "No, I was not aware." He turned and walked to the Chev. As he turned on the engine and pulled away, he wondered what he was going to say when he picked up Harper, Andrea, and Madeline at Pages Books on Kensington where they were scheduled to meet.

×

Lane and Harper walked into the Vietnamese restaurant three hours later. The man they were looking for sat at the back, where he could see every other patron as well as outside onto the street separating Chinatown from the federal building.

The man with the white hair looked up from his bowl of soup. Rice noodles and a thin slice of rare beef hung from his chopsticks. He set the noodles back into his bowl, waved the two detectives over, and waited.

They sat down on either side of the man, who was dwarfed by the detectives. Their body language implied deference.

"Detective Lane. Detective Harper." The man waited.

"Uncle Tran, we have a favour to ask." Harper squeezed his hands together.

"Are you hungry?" Uncle Tran asked.

"Yes," Lane said.

"It's difficult to talk on an empty stomach." Uncle Tran waved at the waiter. "Order first."

Uncle Tran steered the conversation away from serious matters with questions about their families and responded to queries about his extensive familial connections until two steaming bowls of soup arrived.

Lane's mouth watered as he looked at the noodles, cucumbers, tomatoes, and beef in coconut milk and satay broth.

Harper took his spoon and sipped broth. His eyes closed. His head leaned back as the pleasure of the moment overtook him.

"You mentioned a favour?" Uncle Tran set his chopsticks down and reached for a cup of tea.

Lane said, "We have two sisters. One is almost eighteen and the other is in kindergarten. The father is being charged with murder and other offences. We got news a few hours ago that their mother died this morning."

Uncle Tran nodded. "This is the dentist who killed the young woman?"

Harper said, "Yes."

"What are the other offences?" Uncle Tran set down his cup of tea.

"It looks like he's part of a child pornography ring and has a partner who used the dental office to launder money from stolen vehicles," Lane said.

"And the children need a lawyer? That is the favour you are about to ask?" Uncle Tran watched the detectives intently.

You're way ahead of us, Lane thought. "Yes and the children will need a good one because of the circumstances their father has placed them in."

Tran smiled. "I'll speak with Tommy. As you know, he has considerable experience in these matters. Are you enjoying your meal?"

"Of course. Now tell us more about Tony, Rosie, Jay, and Cole," Harper said.

Tran laughed. "There is much to tell."

×

"You promise to stay in touch?" Alexandra asked as she stood at the entrance to US customs.

"I will." Christine had been quiet for the entire drive to the airport.

Lane watched her as she hugged Alexandra. *I wonder how she's taking this. Finding a sister and then saying goodbye.*

Alexandra kissed Christine on the cheek before hugging Lane and Arthur. She said to Lane, "Take good care of my sister." Alexandra hefted her carry-on bag and waved goodbye before turning the corner and disappearing behind the opaque sliding glass door.

Christine smiled at her uncles, "Thank you."

×

Stockwell looked up when Harper and Lane entered the waiting room outside Chief Smoke's office. Stockwell cocked his head to the left to indicate they should sit, then tapped a message on his computer.

Lane looked at the walls newly adorned with photographs of Smoke shaking hands with an extensive variety of the city's who's who. Lane spotted one of Smoke and Bishop Paul. Smoke was smiling into the camera and shaking hands with the bishop.

Harper followed Lane's gaze, made eye contact with his partner, and rolled his eyes.

"Chief'll see you now," Stockwell said.

Lane glanced over his shoulder on his way to the door and saw that Stockwell was back to playing solitaire. "Winning yet?"

Lane opened the door to see Chief Calvin Smoke sitting behind his desk. He didn't stand as they came in. He was on the phone and gestured that the detectives should sit down. Then he rotated his chair so that his back was to them.

Lane looked at the photographs on the wall by the window. A picture of Smoke shaking hands with the mayor had replaced the picture of Smoke, Bishop Paul, and Dr. Jones.

"Of course," Smoke said, then hung up and swung back to face them. He stood up, came around the front of the desk, and sat on the edge with one foot on the ground and the other swinging from the knee. He frowned at the detectives.

Lane caught the scent of aftershave, breath freshener, and alcohol.

Smoke smiled. "What do you have on Dr. Jones?"

Lane and Harper looked at each other.

Instinctively, Lane spoke in monotone. "Jones' partner confessed that the doctor murdered Jennifer Towers. An independent witness, the border guard, told local authorities that Doctor Jones was involved in child pornography. Jones' stepdaughter revealed that Jones sexually assaulted her over a period of five years, starting when she finished kindergarten. There is also evidence from Dr. Jones' laptop of him sedating prepubescent female patients, photographing them, and trafficking the images on the Internet."

Lane watched as Smoke glanced to where the photograph of him and Dr. Jones once hung on the wall. Smoke put both feet on the ground, went back behind his desk, and said, "I see."

Lane waited and thought, *Cam, keep your mouth shut.*

Smoke looked at Lane. "I hear you enjoyed your nephew's performance at the play the other night."

Lane thought, *Why does this sound like another threat?* He nodded.

"And your niece is doing well?" Smoke smiled.

He has, Lane thought, *a predatory smile.*

"I believe your partner's name is Arthur. He is well?" Smoke asked.

"Is that all sir?" Lane asked.

"Yes, detectives, you are dismissed."

Harper lead the way out, past Stockwell and out to the hallway, where they waited for the elevator.

Harper looked at Lane, who refused to make eye contact.

They rode the elevator in silence and stayed that way until they got inside of the Chev.

"What the hell was that all about?" Harper started the engine.

"Our new police chief is not very pleased. We arrested a member of the scotch drinkers' club and embarrassed some very powerful people. We embarrassed Smoke. This won't be forgotten," Lane said.

"Why did he ask about Matt, Christine and Arthur?" Harper backed the vehicle up.

"I think it was a threat. A veiled threat that he can get close to my family any time he wants to," Lane said.

"Shit!" Harper looked ahead and shifted into drive. "The chief warned me about Smoke."

"This situation reminds me of an old curse," Lane said.

Harper looked right at oncoming traffic and waited for an opening. "Well?" he asked.

"May you live in interesting times."

Acknowledgments

Bruce, for caring for us for all these years, and for recommending yearly mammograms, thank you.

Officer Justine: thanks for answering odd questions.

Again, thanks to Tony Bidulka and Wayne Gunn.

Karma, Alex, Sebi, and Bryce: thanks for the skilled editing of scenes.

Doug, Lou, Natalie, Loretta, NJ, Tiffany, and Paul: thank you for all that you do.

Thanks to the burgeoning creative writers at Nickle, Bowness, Lord Beaverbrook, Alternative, Forest Lawn and Queen Elizabeth high schools.

Sharon, Karma, Ben, Luke, Meredith, and Indiana. What can I say? I am blessed.

Garry Ryan was born and raised in Calgary, Alberta. He received a BEd and a diploma in Educational Psychology from the University of Calgary, and taught English and creative writing to junior high and high school students until he retired in 2009. That same year, Ryan received the Calgary Freedom of Expression Award in recognition of his outstanding contributions to the local arts community.

Ryan's debut Detective Lane novel, *Queen's Park* (2004), sprang from a desire to write a mystery that would highlight the unique spirit and diverse locations of his hometown. The follow-up, *The Lucky Elephant Restaurant* (2006), won the 2007 Lambda Literary Award for Best Gay Mystery. *A Hummingbird Dance* (2008) helped cement a loyal following for Ryan's books in North America and overseas. Look for Detective Lane to face a new set of challenges, both as a police officer and as a family man, in *Malabarista,* the forthcoming fifth book in the series.